MORE STORIES OF THE *Rich* AND *Famous*

AIKEN'S WINTER COLONY IN THE GILDED AGE

David M. Lavernier

To Quinn & Meagan
Enjoy the stories!

Dave McLauren

outskirtspress

DENVER, COLORADO

More Stories of the Rich and Famous
Aiken's Winter Colony in the Gilded Age
All Rights Reserved.
Copyright © 2014 David M. Tavernier
v2.0

Cover photo - *"Mrs. Hitchcock prepares to lead the hunt."* Courtesy of Aiken County Historical Museum. Used with permission.

Outskirts Press, Inc.
http://www.outskirtspress.com

ISBN: 978-1-4787-4003-2

Outskirts Press and the "OP" logo are trademarks belonging to Outskirts Press, Inc.

PRINTED IN THE UNITED STATES OF AMERICA

To Mrs. Polly Tecklenburg Durban in appreciation of her forty years of dedication to the Aiken Preparatory School.

CONTENTS

FOREWORD

In the first place, David Tavernier is a good, entertaining writer. Perhaps equally important, he is an energetic, meticulous, ravenous researcher. He is in love with his hometown of Aiken, South Carolina—as well he should be, because it is a charming town. Indeed, some of the early glitterati, the Winter Colony, as they were known, residents and visitors alike, insisted on it being just that…or they wouldn't have been here.

When you combine the colorful characters of the Gilded Age, up through the Roaring Twenties into the days of World War II, then weave them into the tapestry of one of their favorite playgrounds—Aiken—you have a picturesque book.

You may think you are pretty much aware of the role that Aiken played in the social life of some of the most glamorous and illustrious families in the history of this nation. But you haven't scratched the surface. In the early days, you could not walk down any of our main drags without running into a Whitney, Hitchcock, Iselin, Astor, Vanderbilt, and…you get the picture. And their comings and goings during those glory days are fascinating, and they are chronicled here.

The lovely thing about *More Stories of the Rich and Famous* is that it is absolutely factual. And fun. I say again, it is painstakingly researched, but not dry. In fact, many of the insights into the pursuits of these people are—to put it mildly—extraordinarily spicy.

You will feel like you were there when the *Titanic* went down (with many Aiken-related people on board). You'll be in on some of the lively banter in the locker room of the Palmetto Golf Club…a spectator at what went on at the Willcox or the Highland Park Hotels. David Tavernier gives you a place at the table, when some of America's "Four Hundred" wined and dined, and deliciously dished the dirt at Joye Cottage.

You'll get a kick out of reading this delightful labor of love by David Tavernier. I am grateful that he wrote it.

W. Cothran (Cot) Campbell
Aiken, South Carolina

PREFACE

In my first book on this subject, *Stories of the Rich and Famous: Aiken's Winter Colony in the Gilded Age,* a more detailed description of Aiken's beginning leading to the establishment of the winter colony is given. The following is offered to provide the uninitiated reader a thumbnail description of the events leading to the founding of the "Winter Colony."

What was to become the city of Aiken began as a place of refuge whereby South Carolina lowcountry planters, particularly after 1790, which marked the beginning of rice planting, sought relief from the annual threat of malaria that came with summer heat. Some traveled to the coast, others inland. Those who traveled inland to the village of Aiken found that at 500 feet above sea level, the highest point between Charleston and the Savannah River, the area offered a comparatively low humidity, mosquito-free environment. Additionally, its Coker and Calico Springs provided a continuous flow of cool, fresh water. Gradually Aiken came to be known for its pine-scented forests and healthy climate.

As Aiken's reputation grew as a health resort, correspondingly its summer population grew throughout the antebellum years.

In 1833, largely for economic reasons, the first railroad running from Charleston to Hamburg,[1] which passed through the area that would be named Aiken in 1835, made its debut. The 136-mile trip from Charleston could now be made in an unprecedented twelve hours. This development enhanced Aiken's growing popularity as a summer-time health resort, and added another dimension—greater economic development.

Having obtained a charter to build his textile mill, William Gregg

---

1   Hamburg, founded in 1821, was located across from Augusta, Georgia, on the South Carolina side of the Savannah River and served as a consolidation point for cotton shipments to the coast. Hamburg is no longer extant.

of Charleston founded the Graniteville Company in 1846 in what would become Aiken County. Raw cotton could now be woven into clothing here rather than being transported to northern textile mills. Gregg's Graniteville Company became an economic engine providing directly and indirectly for home construction, stores, churches, and other businesses. Additionally, Gregg had personally acquired 5,000 acres on Kalmia Hill in Aiken which he subdivided and sold off to friends who built homes there. By 1855, Gregg all but abandoned Charleston and made his home at Kalmia.

In addition to The Graniteville Company, kaolin mining began in the area. Kaolin is a white type of clay that is used in pottery and porcelain production. In 1856, The Southern Porcelain Company was founded and began to operate in the area, providing employment and a further expansion of the local economy.

By 1861, at the outbreak of the War Between the States, Aiken was well-known to many lowcountry planters and their families. As the war ravaged many areas of the South, Aiken, which had been established for twenty-six years, remained comparatively unscathed with a singular clash occurring in February 1865. At that time, Union Lt. General Hugh Judson Kilpatrick was sent by his commanding general, William T. Sherman, on a mission to burn and destroy the Confederate armory in Augusta, with a further order to disrupt and destroy Confederate infrastructure encountered, including railroad track, in his path while making the loop through Aiken en route to Columbia. When Fitzpatrick arrived on the outskirts of Aiken on February 12th with his 2,000 Union troops, he was unaware that Confederate General Joseph Wheeler,[2] in command of forty-five hundred Confederates, had deployed and was awaiting his arrival.

The Battle of Aiken took place on February 12–13, 1865 and ended in a stalemate with Union forces withdrawing, leaving Aiken untouched by the flame. Union troops did, however, destroy railroad track between Aiken and Blackville, the path of their retreat. The Battle

---

2   Now on either side of the conflict, Kilpatrick and Wheeler have been described as "frenemies," as they were classmates at West Point prior to the War.

of Aiken ended the city's role as a venue of conflict, and the War ended in that same year.

In the wake of the conflict, many lowcountry planters were ruined by the devastation brought on by the War. Their homes, farms, and possessions were destroyed in many cases, and the annual summer migration to Aiken was no longer possible.

The War represented a significant dividing line, demarcating Aiken's past and setting the stage for Aiken's future. It would now acquire a new clientele seeking winter rather than summer refuge.

Since its beginning in 1833, the railroad's network continued to expand, and by War's end, passengers could travel from Aiken to the northeast or to points southeast into Florida, which facilitated the changes that were about to take place.

Postbellum newspapers began to tout Aiken's reputation as a health resort, but now the marketing effort was directed to the north, where the city's reputation and allure were introduced and began to grow. In one such case, Mr. James C. Derby,[3] an influential New York publisher with business connections from Albany to Manhattan, became an early northern property owner. In 1868, Derby came to Aiken and bought a fruit farm from John E. Marley, a prominent Aiken citizen. Derby was among an early group of northern "pioneers" who "discovered" Aiken and believed that it had significant growth potential. Derby was also in a position to promote Aiken to fellow New Yorkers and other northeasterners.

Another postwar early investor in Aiken was Benjamin Chatfield of Waterbury, Connecticut. Almost simultaneous with Derby's arrival, Chatfield, who was a stonemason by trade and president of the Plymouth Granite Company, came to Aiken with a group of investors and began the planning and construction of the Highland Park Hotel. The Highland Park was to become a luxury health resort, attracting some of the country's wealthiest northerners seeking a pleasant, healthy environment and respite from harsh northern winters.

---

3   In 1884, Derby published reminiscences of his life in *Fifty Years Among Authors, Books and Publishers.*

In 1877, Celestine Eustis, of New Orleans and Beverly Farms, Massachusetts, brought her ten-year-old niece, Louise Eustis, to Aiken. Celestine was a member of America's aristocracy, with roots in Louisiana and ties to Washington, D.C. Celestine had already known about Aiken's curative environment, had purchased property on Laurens Street, and began taking her niece there to help relieve "breathing problems," an ailment that seemed to run in the Eustis family.[4]

Celestine would continue to increase her real estate holdings in Aiken during the last half of the nineteenth century as she and Louise would make their annual winter visits. During this time Aiken began to attract more wealthy northerners, and the city prospered and grew. New hotels and boardinghouses were built to accommodate winter guests. Specialty shops and grocers catered to the new visitors' wants and needs.

In 1891, at the age of twenty-four, Louise Eustis married a wealthy sportsman from Westbury, New York, named Thomas Hitchcock. Hitchcock had been educated at Oxford, had taken part in steeplechase and polo there, and became known for his prowess in equestrian sports and skill as a horse trainer both in England and New York.

Shortly after their marriage, as a concession to his new wife, Hitchcock visited Aiken and found the area to have an environment very conducive to training horses. This combined with a mild climate from fall to spring would extend the polo season and simultaneously give respite from the harsh northern winters.

Word of Hitchcock's newly found "winter haven" spread quickly within northeastern equestrian and societal circles, creating the start of an annual northern migration to Aiken.

Ms. Eustis and the Hitchcocks, more than anyone else, using their societal, equestrian, and personal connections in New York and other areas of the northeast, are credited with instigating the annual winter migration to Aiken of some of the wealthiest and most powerful

---

4   Before arriving with her niece, Celestine had already recommended Aiken to her brother, James, who also experienced breathing issues. Additionally, Louise's parents both died from consumption (tuberculosis) while living in France during the War years.

families in the country. And for fifty years it would continue and shape the course of the city's future, culturally and economically, and form the basis of some traditions which continue to this day. The group making up this annual migration would come to be called the "Winter Colony."

∽⟳⟲∾

What took place in Aiken was not unique, as certain other South Carolina cities attracted wealthy northerners in the postwar years. However, nowhere else was this movement greater than in Aiken. Additionally, nowhere else could boast the eminent names, from the highest levels of American society, that came to Aiken. Such wealth and power associated with the names Astor, Whitney, McLean, Harriman, Iselin, Vanderbilt, among numerous others, owned or leased homes in Aiken every winter season.

Foreign royalty came, such as former King Edward VIII, who became duke of Windsor following his abdication, and his wife, Wallis Simpson, duchess of Windsor; Russian Prince Alexis Obolensky of the Rurik Dynasty, an émigré to the U.S. following the Soviet takeover in 1917; Swedish Count and Countess Bernadotte, who were from a line of princes denied accession to the throne due to morganatic marriage.

Political giants came, such as British Prime Minister Winston Churchill; President Franklin D. Roosevelt, who would lodge at Aiken's Willcox Hotel, and William Howard Taft, who would play golf at Aiken's Palmetto Golf Club. Numerous state and U.S. senators from around the country came to Aiken, including Nicholas Longworth, Speaker of the U.S. House of Representatives (1925–1931), who was to die at a friend's home on Hayne Avenue.

Entertainer and columnist Will Rogers came to Aiken to learn polo from Mrs. Hitchcock. Singer Andy Williams found his true love in Aiken and purchased the W. R. Grace estate. Fred Astaire and Paul Newman would come to visit an aunt and a mother-in-law. And Bing

Crosby loved to play golf at the Palmetto Golf Club.

Along with entertainers came world-class musicians bearing the names Josef Hofmann, Efrem Zimbalist, Pablo Casals, and Leopold Stokowski. Operatic divas Marcella Sembrich, Frederika Von Stade, and the famous tenor Enrico Caruso came as well. Some would stay in Aiken for years; others were annual visitors or invited guests.

Iconic names in golf played at Aiken's celebrated Palmetto Golf Club, including Bobby Jones, Sam Snead, Harry Vardon, Byron Nelson, Ben Hogan, Henri Picard, and Jimmy Demaret, among others.

Names associated with the corporate and business world came and built or bought cottages that could more accurately be described as mansions, including Eugene Grace, president of Bethlehem Steel; William Zeigler, president of Royal Baking Powder Company; Seymour Knox of F. W. Woolworth Co.; Robert R. McCormick, president of the *Chicago Tribune*; and F. Ambrose Clark, grandson of the founder of Singer Sewing Machine Company. These represent a small sampling of the industrial wealth that came to Aiken primarily to enjoy equestrian sports throughout the winter.

In *More Stories of the Rich and Famous: Aiken's Winter Colony in the Gilded Age,* I have sought to place the reader in the action as a witness to certain events that enmeshed Aiken's rich and famous. In "Aiken Remembers the *Titanic*," Madeleine Astor describes her recurring nightmare during a visit to Aiken to attend an Augusta bridge dedication to one of *Titanic's* victims. In "Titanic Bill," the story of pitiable William Carter, a *Titanic* survivor, mulls a sad option designed to restore his damaged reputation. In "The Highland Park Hotel," the grandest hotel of its day, the reader learns about its builder, the people who made it run, and the immediate hours leading up to its destruction by fire in the early morning of February 6, 1898. All was not sunshine and roses for Aiken's rich and famous as "Aiken's Trial of the Century" reconstructs in as much detail as is known the attempted murder of wealthy socialite Camilla Havemeyer Beach on the night of February 26, 1912. In "Tommy Hitchcock, Jr. — A Soldier's Story," we learn about Aiken's hometown war hero, his daring escape from a German POW train, and his experiences defending France in the WW I Lafayette Flying Corps. "The Remarkable Iselins" recounts C. Oliver Iselin's 1893 America's Cup victory despite dealing with gale-force winds, his marriage to Hope Goddard, and her involvement in bringing Aiken's first hospital into reality in 1917. The little known story of Representative Nicholas Longworth's 1931 visit to Aiken is recounted in "The Speaker's Final Visit to Aiken," perhaps the most unique among the tales.

In creating the stories, choosing the subjects presented a challenge due to the many that could have been chosen. I believe that the reader of Aiken's history will find those presented to be unique and interesting; however, because those individuals' lives and activities commanded a much wider stage than that offered by Aiken, their stories would appeal to any reader who may enjoy witnessing the activities and travails of the rich and famous.

Because each story is independent and designed to stand on its own, there is no particular order in which they should be read.

As in my earlier effort, all people and places in these stories are real. Nearly all of the events actually took place. Employing reasonable conjecture, I have tried to recreate what may have been said by the characters based upon what is known about those events. As such, this work falls into the category of historical fiction.

It is with deep appreciation and thanks to my dear friends W. Cothran (Cot) Campbell, president of Dogwood Stables, for taking the time from his busy schedule to write the foreword, and Robert J. "Bob" Harrington, Headmaster Emeritus, Aiken Preparatory School, for reviewing the stories and giving his comment.

I am grateful to my good friend Allen Riddick, president of the Aiken County Historical Society, for loaning me a very rare photo, and his overall words of encouragement.

For archival photos and access to the historical records at the Aiken County Historical Museum, my sincerest thanks to former Executive Director Elliott Levy, and Mary White. And for encouragement and advice, I extend my thanks to Owen Clary, Chairman of Aiken County

Historical Commission.

For photos of the Iselin family, I owe thanks and appreciation to Ms. Lisa Hall, supervisor of the Aiken Thoroughbred Racing Hall of Fame and Museum.

And lastly, but certainly not least, my heartfelt thanks to my dear wife, Patrice, for patiently reading, and re-reading my manuscript, making valuable suggestions as the work evolved.

David M. Tavernier
Aiken, South Carolina

AIKEN REMEMBERS
THE *TITANIC*

April 14, 1914

It is now well past three in the morning, and after two years I am still plagued by the chronic insomnia that was brought about by that most awful of nights. My sleeplessness is further aggravated by being here alone, except for my two-year-old son, in Jack's[5] Aiken home.[6] I call it his home because he shared it with Ava,[7] his previous wife, and because of the night that could have only been conceived in hell, we will never spend one winter or spring here together. Nevertheless, I have never been more certain of anything in my life. The horror I continue to experience in late night hours stems from the night of 14 April 1912. I remember it as if it took place last night.

It was after one in the morning that Jack took my maid Rosalie,[8] my nurse Caroline,[9] and me up to *Titanic's* gymnasium, where we waited to board a lifeboat. On the boat deck, crew members were feverishly unlashing lifeboats, while a senior officer repeatedly megaphoned, "Women and children only in the lifeboats, please!" As we waited in silence before lifeboat Number 4, I could feel the ship begin listing to port. It was a clear, cloudless night with millions of stars shining brightly. And indeed, one would have thought it was New Year's Eve as the white, sparkling rockets were being continuously launched into the night sky from the bridge deck. It was cold, as evidenced by everyone's

---

5   John Jacob Astor IV was known as "Jack" to his friends and family.
6   Astor's home was located on the corner of Colleton Avenue and Union Street, directly across the street from the Vanderbilt home.
7   Ava Lowle Willing married John Jacob Astor IV in 1891. After a tumultuous marriage, they divorced in 1909 with Astor's admission of adultery.
8   Rosalie Bidois was Madeleine Astor's maid and companion.
9   Because Madeleine Astor was five months pregnant, Caroline Endres accompanied the couple on their honeymoon cruise to Europe.

breath streaming like smoke with every quickening exhalation, but the dreadful reality of the disaster unfolding before us rendered my limbs and face impervious to the North Atlantic's frigid bite. I raised my eyes to the ink-black sky, partially to avoid seeing the mad rush of passengers running to and fro, some clutching children, some weeping, others shouting names in anguished desperation, searching for lost family members, and partially to avoid the sight of the freezing black water that continued to rise as *Titanic's* list became more acute. Jack had helped me into the cork-filled life jacket before he firmly but gently lifted me into the lifeboat when our turn came.

"What about Kitty?" he asked as I took my seat. With that question, the senior officer in charge again shouted what now had become a warning, "Women and children only in the lifeboat, please!"

During earlier loadings, some first-class male passengers and a few pets were allowed to enter the lifeboats, but no longer. Even Jack's request to accompany me due to my pregnancy fell on deaf ears. My beloved Airedale, Kitty, was to stay behind with Jack and hope for the best.

I will never forget what would be the last words he would ever say to me as he firmly clasped my hand in his as the crewmen began to lower lifeboat Number 4 down *Titanic's* side. "The sea is calm, you'll be all right. You're in good hands. I'll see you in the morning."[10] Our eyes met and held as the pulleys began to squeal under the steady strain of the ropes taking us down what used to be six stories to the rising, icy water.

As we passed E deck, we heard the desperate, frantic cries of third-class passengers begging to be let up to the lifeboat deck, hoping to get a seat. We could see the ship's head taking on water as people ran toward the stern in a futile attempt to escape the rising ocean. Only a few feet away, we looked face-to-face into the eyes of desperate men standing on the deck's rail, who, having been denied lifeboat seats, stood staring straight out with bug eyes and jumping to a certain hypothermic death

---

10   Sources differ on Astor's last words to his wife. An alternate source reports that he stated, "Good-bye, dearie, I'll join you later."

in the freezing water waiting below.

As we continued our descent, and before reaching the water, we were seized with horror when, in the blink of an eye, the woven cords of the overburdened davit ropes began to unravel and spin apart, and in an instant we dropped the final distance into the water with such a jaw-slamming thud that I thought it would crack the hull of our little boat. My heart leapt into my throat.

After regaining my composure, I realized my good friend from Philadelphia, Eleanor Widener,[11] and her maid were sitting with their backs to me on the seat ahead. She, her husband George, and her twenty-seven-year-old son Harry were returning from a trip to Paris, where they were seeking to hire a chef for their new Philadelphia hotel, the Ritz Carlton. A consummate bibliophile,[12] Harry had made a side trip to London in the hope of adding more rare books to his already prodigious collection.

Father and son remained on the ship.

I also noticed Lucille Carter[13] of Philadelphia and her two children, who were seated at the opposite end of the lifeboat; curiously, her young son William wore a ladies' hat.

As we moved away from the big ship's flank, *Titanic's* lights were still glowing, and we could see the Widener men and Mr. Carter huddling with Jack on the first-class aft deck, which slowly continued to rise ever higher, as *Titanic's* head was now completely awash by the relentlessly rising sea.

It was now about two in the morning of 15 April and around our little boat we saw and heard the desperate wails of those who had leaped, some clinging to jetsam and others flopping about in the water begging to be picked up. Those with enough command of their freezing limbs

---

11   Eleanor Elkins Widener married George D. Widener in 1883. She was the daughter of Widener's father's business partner in the Philadelphia Traction Company, U.S. Steel, and American Tobacco Company.

12   Although he was just twenty-seven years of age, Harry Widener had already amassed a sizeable collection of rare books, including an original Guttenberg Bible. In his pocket at the time of the sinking was a rare copy of Bacon's *Essaies*, edition of 1598, which he had purchased before leaving London.

13   Lucille was the wife of "Titanic Bill" Carter, an Aiken winter colonist who was to become infamous following the disaster.

were trying to swim to the lifeboats. Those who came close met with the coxswain's oar, beating them away for fear of being swamped. Some succeeded and clung to our gunwales any way they could. Amid the sometimes excruciating shrieks and faint cries and sobs, we could still hear Mr. Hartley's[14] musicians playing sprightly tunes on the upper deck. What a macabre mix of dying wail and ragtime tunes, I thought, as my mind tried to cope with the hellishly dreadful scene before us that could have been scripted by Dante.

It was cold and I shivered almost uncontrollably. I covered my ears to drown out the cries of the dying and the thrashing sound of those black-eyed, pale blue victims frantically trying to swim to nowhere. I fixed my eyes on *Titanic's* upper deck as we continued to make progress away from the ship's now vertically ascending stern.

Although we were fifty or more yards from the ship's sinking head, I now saw a fifth man join our group of men on deck. He was in full military uniform, and I could clearly tell that it was Major Archibald Butt, who had served as military aide to President Theodore Roosevelt and now to President Taft. He was a native of Augusta, Georgia, and Jack, Mr. Carter, Mr. Widener, and Harry knew him well from their trips to Aiken. I tried to imagine what sort of conversation might be taking place among them as they must certainly now know that their chances for survival were severely diminished.

I tapped my friend Eleanor on the shoulder. She turned, began a timid grin, and immediately I could see tears begin to well up.

"Madeleine, I am so happy to see you. I had no idea that you were on this same lifeboat. We must have missed one another in the confusion when they were loading," she said, while making a labored half turn to embrace me.

"Do you see our men, together there, on the first-class deck?" I asked as I pointed to the ever-diminishing figures on one of the uppermost decks of the ship.

---

14   Hartley led an orchestra consisting of: Jock Hume, violinist; Mr. Taylor, pianist; Fred Clark, bass viol player; Mr. Woodward, cellist, and three others named Brailey, Krins, and Breicoux. They divided into two groups and played ragtime on deck to keep spirits up. They all perished in the sinking and were later hailed as heroes by many in the media.

Before Eleanor could respond, there came a loud, dull screech accompanied by the crunch of breaking steel and the whip-like zing of snapping cables as they were torn from the funnels. With our disbelieving eyes, we watched the forward half of *Titanic* break apart and begin to plunge nose first, darkening its lights and taking two of its great stacks with it, into the open maw of a hungry ocean. In response, the great ship's stern dropped from its near vertical position flat down to the surface. The impact of its slam was so great that it created a widening circle of foam-topped waves and wavelets, which we could now see rolling toward our little boat. All sat in stunned awe of the sight we had just witnessed!

The rear half of *Titanic* momentarily lay flat on the ocean's surface as it hung by a steel thread to its forward section, which had now begun its descent to the ocean floor. Despite the darkness, we could discern seawater begin to fill the ship through its exposed midsection, and those left aboard, responding to the survival instinct, were now scrambling to the ship's stern. We could see deck furniture, equipment, and bodies sliding and falling toward the now sinking midsection. We could no longer see our men on the upper deck. Eleanor began to quietly weep.

I glanced at my timepiece, and it showed fifteen minutes after two. *Titanic's* rear half, which was moments ago flat on the ocean's surface, standing still, began a slow descent. It was, at this point, impossible to hope for any happy outcome for those left on board. Mr. Hartley's music was now silenced and replaced by the rise and fall of the weeping wail coming from the many bobbing heads visible against the dark outline of the sinking second half of *Titanic*.

It was now two-twenty in the morning, and every eye in our little boat was fixed on what little could still be seen of the doomed ship. We heard a loud, bubbling swoosh of ocean as *Titanic's* giant propellers, now facing the black sky, followed the stern, creating a swirling whirlpool within an enveloping sea, swallowing its human and steel prey together as would a behemoth from the deep.

Within an hour of the sinking, there was total silence except for the lapping of wavelets against the side of our small boat. Because there was no moon that night, our vision was faint, but nonetheless we could discern a silent, floating graveyard. Men, women, and children in life vests, some bobbing like corks in a ghostly dance, others facedown, while others floated frozen with a death grip on whatever flotsam they could grasp in a futile attempt to escape the frigid water.

It was early dawn, approximately four in the morning, when the Cunard Liner *Carpathia* arrived on the scene. *Carpathia's* Captain Rostron had heard our distress calls some four hours earlier and immediately raced the fifty-eight miles, dodging icebergs and ice fields in the darkness, in his rush to our aid.

As the images of that horrid night fade, my chronic nightmare ends, and I find myself still sleepless in the upstairs bedroom of our Aiken home. I hear young John Jacob VI[15] begin to stir in the next room. As the first light of dawn comes through my window, I can see the glow of electric lights emanating from the bedroom windows of the Vanderbilt home across Colleton Avenue.

I think about Jack and the short time we had together as husband and wife, and I am sad that he was never to see his son born, but somehow, I am comforted by the fact that there will be some sense of immortality for him through this child.

It was only four years ago[16] that I met John Jacob Astor IV. It was in the summer at Bar Harbour, where he had invited my parents, William Hurlburt Force and Katherine Arvilla Talmage,[17] to a picnic. Father knew John Jacob from his business, William H. Force and Company, a shipping and manufacturing concern founded by my grandfather in Brooklyn.

At the time of our meeting, Jack had been divorced from his wife, Ava, for one year. As I've come to understand it, his divorce was a sort

---

15 Madeleine's two-year-old son, born four months after the *Titanic* sinking, was named John Jacob Astor VI. Although his father was John Jacob IV, his cousin, William Astor, had already named his son John Jacob V when he was born in 1886.

16 Madeleine Talmage Force was seventeen years of age when she met John Jacob Astor IV in 1910. He was forty-five.

17 Daughter of Thomas Tulmage, former mayor of Brooklyn, NY.

of manumission from an overbearing woman who dwelt on improving her social position more than anything else.[18] Ava Lowle Willing Astor had come from Philadelphia and had familial roots in the city's political and judicial systems. Although the marriage was tumultuous, she gave Jack two children: William Vincent,[19] born in 1891, and Ava Alice Muriel,[20] born in 1902. Jack's only enjoyment in life was being with his son, Vincent. They often spent time together aboard the Astor yacht, or anywhere Ava was not.

Although I never thought so, Jack was considered awkward and slow-witted by both his family and the national press. He was treated poorly and was not accepted into Ava's societal circle. He often took meals alone, on a tray, while Ava entertained society friends in another part of their palatial Fifth Avenue, New York home. However, he was able to change that false public image to a great extent with the coming of the Spanish-American War in 1898. He was patriotic and always harbored admiration for the military image, and the war provided him an opportunity to indulge his predilection for the military lifestyle.

Following the explosion on the battleship *Maine* in Havana Harbor, which launched the war against Spain, Jack loaned his yacht, *Nourmahal*,[21] to the U.S. Navy, and they gladly accepted it for wartime use. Additionally, he spent $75,000[22] to finance an entire 100-man army artillery battery equipped with field guns, so called the "Astor Battery," which was destined for action in Cuba and the Philippines. Jack accompanied the battery to Cuba and was given the rank of lieutenant colonel, a title he cherished and preferred since that time.

My attention is now drawn to sounds coming from John Jacob's bedroom. He has awakened and I can hear my maid Rosalie's soothing voice reassuring him as she prepares him for his morning bath.

---

18   Ava lived in the shadow of her mother-in-law, Caroline Astor, who was the undisputed matriarch of New York society.

19   Vincent became the chief beneficiary of Astor's will, receiving $69 million ($1.7 billion in today's currency), including the Astor estate in Rhinebeck and his yacht, *Noma*.

20   Ava Alice Muriel received a $10 million ($246 million in today's currency) trust fund from Astor's will.

21   *Nourmahal* was 250 feet long and 745 tons. Astor also gave free transportation to troops and volunteers on his Illinois Central Railroad.

22    $2,083,000 in today's currency.

Today is a special day. My friend Eleanor Widener will be arriving about noon in Aiken from Philadelphia in her private Pullman. I have not seen her since the disaster at sea, and we are reunited here by invitation of former President and Mrs. Taft to attend the dedication of the Major Archibald Butt Bridge in Augusta. The president's personal secretary called to extend the invitations to Eleanor and myself, not because we are survivors of the *Titanic* sinking, but because our husbands were good friends with Major Butt, and they shared the same end.

President Taft regarded and treated Butt as a son or brother, and used his influence to energize a movement to memorialize the major for his service to our country. In addition to the bridge memorial, three additional memorials have either been completed or are in the process of being established: one at Arlington National Cemetery, a second, the Butt-Millet Memorial Fountain[23] on the Ellipse in Washington, and a third, in the Washington National Cathedral.

Archibald Butt came from a line of military men. His grandfather, Archibald Butt, served in the American Revolutionary War, and his great-grandfather, Josiah Butt, was a lieutenant colonel in the Continental Army. His uncle was General William R. Boggs, who served in the Confederate States Army. As I had only just met him on the *Titanic* during the voyage, I didn't know the major well, but Jack admiringly spoke of him often, so it is through Jack that I have come to know some of his history. Today, we will be attending the dedication of the Archibald Butt Memorial Bridge in Augusta with President and Mrs. Taft. And this evening Eleanor, her son George Jr., and I have all been invited by Harry Payne Whitney[24] to his home, Joye Cottage, for dinner and entertainment.

---

23   Butt's companion with whom he shared his home in Washington was Francis Davis Millet. Millet was with Butt at the time of the sinking and was also lost. Millet was an artist/painter and along with Butt was known for the large parties they hosted that were attended by members of Congress, Supreme Court Justices, and the President himself.

24   Eldest son of William C. Whitney, Harry took possession of the Aiken home in 1904 through inheritance. Additionally, his share of the estate was $11.5 million, about $283 million in today's currency.

✐

Eleanor Widener checked her timepiece. It was now 11:15 a.m. and she would be arriving at the Aiken Station at 12:30 p.m., just as her steward had predicted. She sat in silence and sipped her tea while listening to the rhythmic clack of the rails pass under the family's custom-built Pullman. She never noticed the fallow cotton fields and rows of fledgling cornstalks pass by, for she thought about how her life had changed these two years since the disaster at sea. She thought about her husband George, and her beloved son Harry, whose bodies, if they were recovered, were unrecognizable. She had learned how to live with a stiff upper lip, something few, if any, northeastern society matrons ever had to do. Two of her men were just memories—empty graves—but she would make certain that they would not be forgotten, especially Harry. To ensure his lasting memory, she had already begun building the Harry Elkins Widener Library at Harvard College.[25] She could think of no better place to house his extensive rare and famous book collection. A consummate bibliophile, Harry had loved his years at Harvard, and she was sure he would approve of Harvard serving as custodian for his beloved volumes.

Wanting to avoid appearing maudlin upon arrival in Aiken, she focused her thoughts on Eleanor[26] and George Jr. *Yes, I still have them, and they will continue to be my lifelong joy.*

The train steward came to collect her empty teacup, and informed her that they would be in Aiken within the next fifteen minutes. With compact in hand, she surveyed her aging features in the Pullman's gilded mirror, patting here and wiping there in a vain attempt to erase the creases that seemed to have become more prominent over the past two years.

George Jr. was already at the station, patiently seated atop his

---

25   Harry had graduated from Harvard in 1907 and was a member of the Owl Club there. His memorial library was dedicated on 2 June 1915.

26   Her daughter Eleanor was born in 1891 and was not aboard the *Titanic* on that fateful night.

four-in-hand,[27] waiting for his mother's arrival. She was not a horse-woman of any sort, and he knew she would prefer being collected with the Mercedes, but he was an equestrian and his thoroughbreds were most important to him, the Mercedes merely a necessary evil.

He was once again in Aiken at the home he perennially leased for the season.[28] In the past his parents, brother, and sister would visit him in Aiken, not because they had interest in thoroughbreds or the fox hunt, but because their friends with whom they enjoyed socializing, the Astors and the Whitneys, always spent time in Aiken each winter. George Jr.'s love of equestrian activities developed through the influence of his uncle, Joseph Early Widener,[29] who had a substantial financial stake in the horse-racing industry.

The Wideners were a tight-knit family, and as so often over the past two years, he thought of his father and missed him dearly; they had been close from his childhood until the tragedy at sea.

George Jr.'s father was fifty years of age when he perished in the sinking. He was the son and heir of P. A. B. Widener[30] of Philadelphia, who began his rise as a merchant supplying meat to the Union Army during the War Between the States. He later made his fortune founding the Philadelphia Traction Company, a public transit streetcar business similar to that operated by William C. Whitney in New York City, and was a founding organizer of U.S. Steel and the American Tobacco Company. George Jr.'s father was P.A.B. Widener's eldest son, who joined him in the streetcar business and was successful in implementing many innovations in the cable and electric streetcar business. When George Jr.'s. father joined his grandfather's business, the Wideners, despite having already accumulated a large fortune, were considered *parvenus* by Philadelphia's societal Brahmins. In 1883, he married Eleanor

---

27   A four-in-hand is a carriage drawn by a team of four horses having the reins rigged in such a way that it can be driven by a single driver. The stagecoach and the tally-ho are examples of four-in-hand coaches.

28   After 1929 he seasonally leased Green Plains (extant) on Whiskey Rd. It was owned by Mrs. Chafee, Eulalie Salley's mother.

29   Joseph Early Widener was head of Belmont Park in NY, and builder of Hialeah Park racetrack in Florida. He maintained thoroughbred stables in Lexington, KY, Florida, and France.

30   P.A.B. Widener (1834–1915) was married to Hannah Josephine Dunton (1836–1896). They had three sons: Harry, George, and Joseph.

Elkins Widener, the daughter of oil and steel financier William Lukens Elkins, one of his father's business partners. George and Eleanor produced three children: Harry (1885), George Jr. (1889), and Eleanor (1891). The family lived at Lynnewood Hall, a 110-room Georgian-style mansion in Elkins Park, Pennsylvania.

When not thinking about his deceased father and brother, George's thoughts frequently returned to the beautiful and somewhat mysterious French lady he had first met in Deauville, France, while attending the races with Uncle Joseph, and a later encounter in New York where he went to meet his mother and to obtain information about his father and brother following the sinking.

The lady, who had also been a passenger on *Titanic*, was a business associate of Coco Chanel[31] and traveled alone using a pseudonym. She and Chanel were in the business of haute couture in Deauville, France, where her fashion designs had been enthusiastically received, allowing a second shop in Biarritz, and a third in Paris on rue Cambon, one of the most fashionable districts of the city. She was also friends with Harry Payne Whitney,[32] whom she also had met in Deauville. George Jr. couldn't help but feel a twinge of excitement about the possibilities as he anticipated seeing Mademoiselle Hattie Forcier[33] again this very evening at Harry Payne's soiree at Joye Cottage.

George Jr. was jolted back from his daydream by the loud whistle of the steam-breathing locomotive, which was now approaching the station. He disembarked the wagon, and amidst the hubbub of porters, cabmen, and freight wagon drivers rushing to the ramp, he excitedly ran onto the platform to greet his mother. He quickly found his father's custom-built railcar as it was easily recognizable with the Widener family crest prominently adorning its blue and gold flanks; the distinctive family colors made the Pullman stand out at any railroad station.

"*Maman, Maman*, I'm here!" George called as he spied her through

---

31 "Coco" was a nickname Chanel acquired in her early years, when she sang in cafés. Her given name was Gabrielle.

32 Harry had taken ownership of Joye Cottage on First & Easy Streets through inheritance following the death of his father, William C. Whitney, in February 1904.

33 Coco Chanel called her friend Adrienne.

the large Pullman viewing window. In her excitement upon seeing her son, Eleanor Widener scampered down the railcar's narrow steps with the vigor of a much younger woman.

"George, how I have missed you. It is so good to see you," she said as she embraced his neck and kissed his cheek. "Aiken must agree with you, as you appear to have gained some weight since I last saw you," she chided, in a playful way.

"Yes, I have been well, *Maman*, and now more so that you have safely arrived," he responded. "I brought my new carriage with my four best draught horses for the ride home," he said in order to prepare her for an accommodation other than the new Mercedes.

Mother and son continued to exchange affectionate greetings as he helped her into the carriage, while the porter stowed the luggage into the rear compartment.

"Well, son, what is the schedule for today's activities? Has Madeleine Astor arrived? What about President Taft?" she asked excitedly, as George turned the horses to begin the short ride home.

"Mrs. Astor has arrived and is at her home on Colleton Avenue. She will be accompanying you to the bridge dedication this afternoon and later to Harry Payne's home for the social gathering. President Taft arrived on the ninth. He is staying at the Bon Air Hotel[34] in Augusta and will be the featured speaker at the bridge dedication since he regarded Major Butt almost as a son. The president has accepted Harry Payne's invitation to join us this evening, so he will be at Joye Cottage also. Harry Payne also invited him to join us tomorrow at the Palmetto Golf Club for a round of golf. Mr. Taft has always loved golf and is playing so much more since he's left office, I'm told," said George.

At three-thirty that afternoon, amidst speeches, exactly two years after the sinking of *Titanic*, the ornate bridge at the corner of Fifteenth and Greene Streets in Augusta was officially dedicated as the Archibald W. Butt Memorial Bridge. Thousands turned out to hear

---

34   Built in 1889, the Bon Air was a lavish winter retreat for wealthy northerners. President Taft stayed at the Bon Air during his golf outings in Augusta and Aiken. Others of note who stayed at the Bon Air include: F. Scott Fitzgerald, President Warren G. Harding, and British Prime Minister Winston Churchill. The Bon Air closed in 1960 as a result of bankruptcy.

the eulogies and witness the dedication. Major Butt was a member of the Temple-Noyes Lodge of Masons in Augusta. It was the Masons who spearheaded the cornerstone ceremony, which was followed by the unveiling. President Taft spoke from the heart without notes as he and Mrs. Taft had been close to Archie, as he was known, since the Theodore Roosevelt administration years, and their time together in the Philippines.

At eight in the evening, guests began arriving at Joye Cottage. Harry Payne and Gertrude Vanderbilt Whitney[35] stood in the cottage's reception area receiving their guests as they were announced by Mr. Whitney's head butler. First to arrive were the widows, Madeleine Force Astor and Eleanor Elkins Widener, who were escorted by George Widener, Jr. Following them came William[36] K. Vanderbilt and his second wife, Anne Harriman Sands Rutherfurd Vanderbilt, who had only recently acquired their Aiken home on Colleton Avenue. They were followed by C. Oliver and Hope Goddard Iselin. Oliver Iselin, who maintained his Aiken cottage, Hopelands, on Whiskey Road, was well acquainted with the Whitney family as fellow members of the New York Yacht Club, and more so since his victories against rivals for America's Cup in 1887 aboard the yacht *Volunteer*, in 1893 with *Vigilant*, and again with the yacht *Columbia* in 1899.

Following the Iselins was the unescorted Mademoiselle Hattie Forcier of Deauville and Paris, France. Mademoiselle Forcier was staying at the Willcox and had made a special trip to Aiken at Whitney's invitation. She had been in New York establishing Coco Chanel's newest American shop, and now she was here, an extremely beautiful woman dressed in the latest Parisian fashion designed by Chanel herself.

She and Chanel were constant companions, attending the races in Deauville,[37] Auteuil, and the many soirees hosted by upper-class

---

35 Harry Payne Whitney and Gertrude Vanderbilt were married on August 25, 1896 at the Vanderbilt summer mansion, the Breakers, in Newport, Rhode Island.

36 William K. Vanderbilt was uncle to Gertrude Vanderbilt Whitney. She was the daughter of William's brother, Cornelius, who had died of a cerebral hemorrhage on September 12, 1899.

37 Chanel became the mistress of Etienne Balsan, a French socialite and heir to a wealthy textile industrialist. He was a polo player and horse breeder and introduced Chanel to the Deauville races. His brother, Louis Jacques Balsan, was to become the second husband of Consuelo

Parisians. She had known Chanel since childhood, when they were both orphaned and in the care of the sisters at Aubazine Convent, associated with the Congregation of the Sacred Heart of Mary in Correze, France. It was during their years together at the convent that they bonded, learned to sew, and experimented with creating different clothing styles. Chanel never forgot her friend Hattie after achieving some business success,[38] and soon she accompanied her everywhere. Their ongoing business collaboration contributed to the increasing success of the Chanel brand. Neither of the women came from the social class within which they now found themselves. Their success, which was brought about by their wildly popular, informally sophisticated, and somewhat provocative women's apparel, evoked a French European mystique and was sought after by upper-class American women. This provided their entrée into American upper-class society.

"*Bonsoir et bienvenue á la maison Joye, Mademoiselle Forcier,*" said Harry Payne in his best Parisian French, as he kissed Hattie's extended hand. Harry had learned the customs of the upper-class French through his many visits to Paris. He did not know her well enough to proffer the double cheek kiss.

"*Je suis enchanté pour être ici, Monsieur Whitney,*" she returned with a provocative smile.

She was in fact thrilled to be there because she knew, as well as Coco Chanel would have known, that there were a number of potential investors for their clothing business present in the room. They never forgot the poverty of their youth; business was always uppermost in their minds, and they knew how to use their female charms to lure wealthy male investors.

Unbeknownst to her at this point, Hattie was being followed with interest by George Widener, Jr. In fact, he'd been surreptitiously eyeing her and dreaming of the possibilities from the moment she entered Joye

---

Vanderbilt in 1921.

38   Through Balsan, Chanel met Captain Arthur Edward Capel, a wealthy member of the English upper class, who became her lover. Capel helped her on the road to success by bankrolling her first shops in Deauville and Biarritz.

Cottage. As she moved through the room exchanging cordialities with old and new acquaintances, George began his drift in her direction.

Whitney's white-gloved domestic staff circulated among the guests with silver trays of the best champagne from Reims, while other staff was seeing to the many sumptuous trays laden with hors d'oeuvres of every kind. Joye Cottage was decorated as never before, mostly in honor of the very special guest expected that evening.

Large stands of tropical flowers and potted palms adorned the foyer and reception hall. The food tables were framed in hydrangea and roses accented by feathery ferns. Everywhere one looked there were reds, blues, greens, and yellows, a virtual rainbow of colors from the many varieties of tropical flowers that adorned the hall.

Even the entertainment was special. Whitney had arranged to take advantage of the fact that the Hofmanns were in Aiken and had special house guests. Knowing this he had asked Joseph Hofmann, "Do you think Dame Sembrich and Maestro Caruso[39] would mind entertaining the president?" Hofmann was so taken aback by the fact that the president would be among the guests that he immediately agreed to provide the accompaniment. He replied that they would be delighted to give a preview of the duet arias from an opera, *La Bohème*, they were scheduled to perform next month at the New York Metropolitan Opera House.

At last, George Widener was within striking distance of Mademoiselle Forcier. As he casually approached, he introduced himself. "Mademoiselle Hattie, I am so happy to see you once again, as it has been some time since we met at the Deauville races. How is Mademoiselle Chanel?" he asked with a broad smile, doing his best to ingratiate himself.

"*Ah, oui, Monsieur George*, it has been a long time; it is so nice to see you again. Coco is well, and our business is well. Coco and I are looking into adding to our product line; we think maybe a perfume,

---

39   Marcella Sembrich, leading international soprano of her day, and Enrico Caruso were already acquainted with the Whitney family. Harry Payne's father had been one of the founders of the NY Metropolitan Opera in 1883 and had brought the pair to New York to perform there in the past.

and we are looking for a name. Do you have any ideas?" she asked coquettishly.

George thought for a moment and asked, "Were you not on *Titanic's* Number Five lifeboat on the night of the sinking?"

"*Mais oui.* I shall never forget when I was placed in lifeboat Number Five that awful night," she returned.

"Well, then, it should be a lucky number for you, and maybe some of that luck will rub off onto your new perfume. Call it simply Number Five," he suggested.

"*Je ne sais pas.* I don't know," she responded with a smile. "I don't know if Coco would like to name her new perfume Number Five. It appears so simple."

"Well, it's just a thought," he returned as he snatched two flutes of champagne from a passing waiter. He handed one to Hattie. "*A votre santé, Hattie!*"

Just as George's conversation with Hattie was beginning to warm up, applause was heard coming from the direction of the cottage foyer, which grew louder as it infectiously rippled through the reception hall and continued unabated as a very rotund, walrus-mustachioed man made his entrance. Murmurs of "*It's the president*" were heard among the gathered guests as each trained his gaze at the small receiving line where the Whitneys were greeting the arrival of William Howard Taft and his wife, Helen Herron Taft.

Taft had gained popularity as Theodore Roosevelt's Secretary of War, an appointment he received as a reward for his campaign efforts on Roosevelt's behalf in 1904. Taft's reputation had grown since his appointment by President McKinley in 1900 to head the commission that established civilian government in the Philippines, which had been ceded to the U.S. following the Spanish-American War. He regarded his presidency, which began in 1908 and lasted for one term, as a springboard for the only office he ever really wanted—Chief Justice of the Supreme Court. Taft was a jurist at heart and a poor politician. For all the offices he had held, his goal was to become a member of the

U.S. Supreme Court.[40]

Not everyone in the hall applauded or was happy with Taft's arrival at Whitney's home. Under his administration the new Sixteenth Amendment to the Constitution, the amendment giving the federal government the authority to collect taxes on income, had been passed and ratified. While many others had a role in promulgating the amendment, Taft received most of the blame. This, combined with his political ineptness, among other circumstances, contributed to his being denied a second term.[41]

After a few moments, Harry Payne called his guests to attention and made the introduction.

"It is my honor and pleasure to introduce to you our country's twenty-seventh president, William Howard Taft," he said as he gestured to Taft for comment.

Taking Harry Payne's cue, Taft began with a somber reminder.

"While it is a pleasure to be in Augusta and Aiken today, it is important that we remember the fine Americans who were lost on this date two years ago, aboard the *Titanic*. I know that there are good people in this room who have been closely affected by that disaster, as I was with the loss of Major Butt, and I would ask for a moment of silence in honor of their memory," he said.

President Taft followed with a short commentary that evening, dwelling on the country's place in the world now that Europe, with its new internal alliances, was heading toward what soon could become a great European war. Taft's comments were followed by polite applause, whereupon he returned to congregate with his host Harry Payne Whitney.

"Well, Harry Payne, how will the Palmetto Club be playing tomorrow?" asked Taft re-engaging his host as the evening's entertainment was about to begin.

---

40 Taft reached his goal on June 30, 1921 when U.S. Supreme Court Justice Edward White died and Taft was nominated to take his place by President Warren G. Harding.

41 In 1912, the Republican vote was split between Taft (25%), and Theodore Roosevelt's Bull Moose Party (27%), which allowed Democrat Woodrow Wilson to win with 41% of the popular vote.

Amidst the glamour, conversations, and introductions among the guests who now filled the reception hall, no one noticed an attractive lady, dressed in the sophisticated fashion of Paris, and a young gentleman slip out the side entrance of Joye Cottage's reception hall into the cool, spring evening…

THE REST OF THE STORY

John Jacob Astor IV's body was recovered from the sea following the tragedy of *Titanic* by the steamer *Mackay-Bennett* on 22 April, eight days following the sinking. It was identified by the jacket he wore that night whose interior lining bore the monogrammed initials *JJA*. In his trousers was found the gold pocket watch he always carried. It is thought that he was killed by one of *Titanic's* falling funnels as the ship began to founder. On his death his estate was valued at $85 million.[42] His son Vincent became the main beneficiary at $69 million, including the Rhinebeck estate and his yacht, *Noma*. His last visit to Aiken predated his 1911 marriage to Madeleine Force.

Madeleine Force Astor's last visit to Aiken was in February 1916 as far as is known. The Astor home, known locally as the Finley Henderson house, is still located today on the corner of Colleton Avenue and Union Street, across from the location of William K. Vanderbilt's Elm Court.[43] From Astor's will Madeleine received $100,000 outright, plus income from a $5 million trust fund[44] along with the use of the Astor home on Fifth Avenue in New York City, all to continue as long as she remained unmarried. Astor's unborn son, John Jacob VI, was left a fund of $3 million.

In June 1916, four months following Madeleine's last known visit to Aiken, she married William Karl Dick, vice president of Manufacturer's

---

42   Based on $85 million, approximately $2 billion in today's valuation. However, estimates of Astor's estate vary from $85 to $125 million depending on the source.

43   Elm Court was owned by the Vanderbilt family 1914–1926. It was destroyed by fire in 1978.

44   Approximately $100 million in today's valuation.

Trust Company, which caused her to lose all benefits left by Astor. She had two sons with Dick, but the marriage did not last and they divorced in July 1933. Four months later, in a foolish rebound, Madeleine married the twenty-six-year-old Italian prizefighter Enzo Fiermonte. The marriage lasted five years.

Madeleine Force Astor Dick died of heart failure in Palm Beach, Florida, on March 27, 1940. Her body was returned to New York, where she was buried in Trinity Church Cemetery, in her mother's mausoleum. She was forty-six years of age.

George D. Widener Sr. and Harry Widener's bodies may have never been recovered following *Titanic's* sinking, as none that were recovered were ever positively identified as either Widener man. George left a large fortune to his wife, Eleanor, son, George Jr., and daughter, Eleanor, who was married only two weeks following her father's death.

Although he was only twenty-seven years of age at the time of his death, Harry Widener had already gained a reputation as a bibliophile and collector of rare books. In his memory, his mother gave his entire collection to his alma mater, Harvard College, where she built the Harry Elkins Widener Memorial Library to house them. That collection can still be seen there today.

Eleanor Elkins Widener, during the dedication ceremony of the Harry Elkins Widener Memorial Library on June 15, 1915, made the acquaintance of Dr. Alexander Rice, a physician and explorer. Before the year had ended, she was married to Dr. Rice and took up world travel with her new husband, visiting exotic places in the East and making many trips to South America's Amazon River basin. Eleanor Widener Rice died of a heart attack in Paris in 1937.

Major Archibald Willingham Butt's body was never recovered from the sea. There were various conflicting accounts given of his last minutes on *Titanic's* deck by survivors who testified at the inquiry following the disaster. Some said he began taking charge and supervised the lowering of the lifeboats, another that he herded women and children into the lifeboats, and yet another, that with "gun in hand," he stopped male passengers from charging the lifeboats. It was said that President Taft broke down, cried, and could not continue the eulogy he was giving during a commemorative ceremony remembering Butt in May 1912.

George D. Widener Jr. continued to visit Aiken each winter. He never owned a home there, but in later years (post 1929) seasonally rented the cottage *Green Plains*[45] on Whiskey Road; however, he did own 7,000 acres on the South Carolina coast. Under the influence of his uncle, Joseph Early Widener, George became a racehorse owner and breeder, and gained a love for all things equestrian.

It is believed that through the influence of his parents' friends William C. Whitney and Thomas Hitchcock, Widener discovered Aiken and began wintering there.

As far as is generally known, George Jr. never again saw Coco Chanel's friend and business partner, Hattie Forcier, following that night in April 1914. In 1917, he went on to marry a wealthy divorcée, Jessie Sloane Dodge, daughter of Henry T. Sloane, a wealthy rug and carpet dealer in New York whose brother William married Emily Vanderbilt—William K. Vanderbilt's sister and daughter of William "Billy" H. Vanderbilt, the Commodore's son.

As a prominent racehorse owner, George Widener, Jr. served as president of the National Museum of Racing and Hall of Fame from 1960 to 1968. He was named "Exemplars of Racing," only one of five so designated by the organization.

He died in 1971 at his Erdheim Farm, Whitemarsh Township,

---

45   Green Plains is extant.

Pennsylvania. His nephew and heir, Fitz Eugene Dixon, Jr., inherited Widener's farm and personal fortune. George was also survived by a stepdaughter, Diana Dodge.

Hattie Forcier's personal and business relationship with Coco Chanel began to disintegrate with Chanel's ten-year affair, beginning in 1923, with Hugh Richard Arthur Grosvenor, the vastly wealthy duke of Westminster, who lavished her with jewelry, art, and a home in London's Mayfair District.

Whether through George Widener's flippant name suggestion or not, indeed, Chanel's *Parfums Chanel* brand introduced Chanel No. 5 fragrance in 1922. As a result of bad negotiations, Chanel gave up most of the ownership and perfume revenue to Pierre and Paul Wertheimer, owners of a large perfume and cosmetics business, in exchange for their financing, production, and marketing of the product that bore her name.

Unable to attract investors, Hattie Forcier never again visited Aiken. After her split with Chanel, her own clothing business endeavors failed. In 1934, she died under unknown circumstances.

Titanic, owned by White Star Lines, was the largest, most powerful and luxurious ship of its day. It struck an iceberg in the North Atlantic on its New York-bound maiden voyage at eleven-forty on the night of April 14, 1912. At two-twenty on the morning of April 15, two hours and forty minutes after striking the berg, she descended twelve thousand feet below the ocean's surface. *Titanic* had 2,223 passengers on board, and of this total 1,517 souls were lost. *Titanic* was, and still is, the greatest civilian maritime disaster in history.

Tommy Hitchcock, Jr.
A Soldier's Story

Germany 1918

It has been seven nights since I scrambled from my dozing German guard and jumped from the prisoner transport train as it rumbled along toward Ulm. I think back to that moment at 10 p.m. when I broke for the railcar door, arousing my captor, and making that perilous jump into the German countryside. Now, I am running and walking at night and hiding during the day. I have become adept at traversing nighttime terrain as my eyes, accustomed through habit, have become efficient in darkness. Although it is somewhat healed, I run fully ignoring the lingering pain in my leg from the German bullet that passed through my thigh when I was shot down during my last dogfight.[46]

I push on powered by thoughts of my family and our home on Laurens Street in Aiken, and my irrepressible desire to evade capture by roving German patrols and be free. Using my rudimentary compass as a means of guidance, I estimate that I have covered some 160 kilometers. Although it is midsummer, I am chilled by the night breeze blowing through my tattered French uniform, wet from the streams that I have forded, as I walk, sometimes run, and other times crawl toward neutral Switzerland. I alternately follow the train's track and the Danube River, avoiding towns and cities as I make my way to the border, which I feel is near. I am almost there.

It is now three o'clock in the morning of the eighth day, and I have reached the Swiss border. I am slowly and quietly making my way to the border crossing, first on my hands and knees through the tall grass,

---

46   On March 6, 1918, Hitchcock, a *pilote de chasse* in France's Lafayette Flying Corps, was shot down as he took on two German Albatrosses. Prior to this engagement, he had two confirmed kills to his credit.

then crawling on my belly through the soft mud, evading searchlights manned by the German checkpoint soldiers stationed in a guardhouse close by, on a rural road. I cross the border through a patch of brush and trees about one hundred yards from the checkpoint. Once safely past the searchlights, I see city lights in the distance, and after a fourth of a mile jog from the frontier, I have found the town of Thayngen, where I have encountered a local policeman.

Breathlessly I spit out, "I am an escaped American prisoner of war seeking asylum!"

With a quizzical stare the policeman asked, "*Quoi? Américain? Mais, je ne comprend pas!*"

I drew a deep breath, thought for a moment, and said, "*Je suis un asile cherchant échappé de prisonnier de guerre américain,*" followed by a silent thanks to Tante Célestine[47] for my childhood French lessons.

"*Ah, oui, américain,*" he said, breaking into a broad smile. "*Suivez moi, s'il vous plaît, monsieur.*"

With newfound energy I followed him to the local jail, where I was offered modest, but well-appreciated hospitality; a hot shower, a warm cot, and the best food I had eaten since landing in a German POW camp. That night I had the soundest sleep I'd had in months!

Born on February 11, 1900 in Aiken, South Carolina, Tommy Hitchcock, Jr. was the third child of Thomas and Louise Eustis Hitchcock. The Hitchcocks were part of the Eastern seaboard aristocracy who maintained homes in Westbury, New York, and Aiken, South Carolina. They, along with Louise's aunt, Celestine, were the founders of Aiken's winter colony—the group that made up the annual migration of wealthy northerners to Aiken each fall.

---

47   Celestine Eustis was Tommy's grand-aunt. She was born in Paris and lived in New Orleans before coming to Aiken. She taught French to Tommy's mother, Louise Hitchcock, and Louise's children during their childhood years in Aiken. The children referred to her as "Tante," meaning "aunt" in French.

Tommy's father was a horse trainer and polo player who made a name for himself competing in English Steeplechase and representing America on the International Polo Team in 1886. He was educated at Oxford and maintained a lifestyle financed mainly by an inheritance from his father, who had been involved in the newspaper business in New York. Tommy's mother was a member of a prominent New Orleans family with ties to the Washington and New England upper classes.

During his childhood, Tommy, always a restless lad, was more attuned to action than theory, and, following his father's example and guidance, began to ride and love horsemanship and polo as a small child. He reveled in feats of juvenile daring, always needing to be the fastest and strongest in games and sports. He always loved a challenge. He was often accused by his sisters of being "Father's Favorite," an accusation that had some truth to it, as Thomas Sr. did indulge his namesake son, whom he wanted to mold in his own image.

Tommy became an expert marksman by the time he was twelve years old, a skill taught to him by his mother in the Aiken preserve.[48] He would find in later years that his developed hand/eye coordination and marksmanship skills would serve him well.

In 1910 he was sent for two years to Fay School, a pre-preparatory academy in Southboro, Massachusetts. In 1912, like many aristocratic New York children, he attended the exclusive preparatory school St. Paul's[49] in Concord, New Hampshire. At school he was an average student, not because he wasn't intellectually competent, but because he easily became bored due to his active nature. Because he had learned French as a young boy, he sometimes had difficulty when writing, mixing French and English words in his sentences, or using a French spelling for an English word of like meaning.

In 1916–1917 Tommy was finishing his time at St Paul's, where he had established a reputation for himself as an outstanding athlete

---

48   The preserve later became known as Hitchcock Woods.

49   A few of the many famous among St. Paul's graduates include: John Jacob Astor, IV of *Titanic* fame; J.P. Morgan, banker and international financier; James R. Garfield, son of President James A. Garfield; and Charles Scribner, III, CEO of Scribner & Son Publishing.

in rowing, shooting, and polo. In his last year at St. Paul's, his natural restlessness was further stimulated by the newspaper accounts he read about the Great War taking place in Europe. He read about the exploits of the special American fighter group called Lafayette Escadrille[50] that was fighting for France, and was fascinated by this relatively new, developing invention, the airplane, which was now being used in warfare. His adventurous nature drove his desire to fly and be part of it. His first choice the U.S. Army Air Corps—was thwarted due to his young age. Moreover, the United States had just committed to joining the conflict, and it would be months, if at any time, before he could become part of the action. He believed that he would need to join the French in order to get into the fight.

After a day of enjoying the cordial hospitality of the people of Thayngen and exchanging cables with *Maman*, with a promise to follow up with a detailed letter of explanation very soon, I boarded the train to Berne to finish recuperating with American family friends Ernest and Lucie Howe Schelling.[51] Mother's return cable provided me with the Schellings' contact information and said how they would be delighted to host my visit until I felt rested enough to return to Paris, where I could inquire about my unit.

Ernest Schelling was born in New Jersey but had spent many years in Europe, studying at the Paris Conservatoire and, prior to that time, the Academy of Music in Philadelphia. He emerged as a world-class pianist, giving performances throughout Europe and North and South America. The Schellings were as comfortable in Switzerland as in New

---

50   By the time Tommy arrived in France, the Lafayette Escadrille had morphed into the Lafayette Flying Corps and was placed under the direction of the French Foreign Legion. This was done to blunt German accusations that the U.S. was no longer neutral since the Corps was made up of Americans. However, now, as Foreign Legionnaires they were considered, in effect, individual mercenaries.

51   The Schellings were friends of certain Hitchcock friends. They knew of the Hitchcocks and offered Tommy a room in their home where he could recuperate from his trying experience.

York, since Ernest had spent so much time there at the Conservatoire and on musical tours.

I settled into my seat for the fifty-mile rail trip to Berne whereupon, still weary from my recent ordeal, I drifted into a sound sleep and began to relive my arrival in France. My groggy doze immediately landed me in Avord.

On the first of July 1917, after spending two weeks in Paris with family friends, Frederik and Dorothy Penrose Allen,[52] who had maintained a home there since 1908, I arrived at l'Ecole Militaire d'Aviation at Avord. It was reputed to be the best military aviation school in the world, and I was about to realize my dream of joining French and American aviators in the Lafayette Flying Corps as a *pilote de chasse*[53] whose exploits, like mounted medieval knights in singular, personal combat on flying steeds, would earn glory for France and praise in the many Franco-sympathetic American newspapers.

Desperate for American military war support, it was in 1916 that the French had created the idea of an American-manned flying corps, and with a flair for public relations named it *Lafayette Escadrille*—a name they knew would find appeal in the adventurous American spirit. Further, it was the French who invented the concept of the *Ace*, a title reserved for those who heroically distinguished themselves in aerial combat with at least five kills.

At Avord I learned the basics of flying in the slower Caudrons and Bleriots,[54] and dreamed of aerial combat school, where I would be given a French-built Nieuport,[55] one of the most advanced fighting aircraft of the time. I was now truly becoming a member of that elite group of pilots.

---

52   Tommy's father had many friends in the publishing business, including Frederik Allen, who was a graduate of Harvard College, had a literary career with *Atlantic Monthly* and *The Century*, and was editor of *Harper's Magazine* for thirty years. He also published several books.

53   Loosely translated — "fighter pilot."

54   Caudrons and Bleriots were used as training aircraft for new pilots and for observation and some bombing in WWI.

55   The Nieuport was a 110 hp WWI aircraft used by French fighter pilots for scouting and aerial combat. It carried a deck-mounted synchronized Vickers gun and made a decisive impact in the aerial war with Germany.

After sixteen weeks of aviation training at Avord, I was *breveted*.[56] Now I was off to Pau, a town in the Pyrenees foothills, for six weeks of aerial combat training. In mid-December 1917, I completed the course and joined my squadron at the front in Luneville, located in Lorraine, the northeastern area of France, where my real and most dangerous odyssey was to begin.

I was awakened with a jolt by the shrill sound of the train's steam whistle as we approached the station at Berne. I opened my eyes and realized that I had missed the entire trip from Thayngen to Berne, where, I was told, some of the most beautiful scenery in Europe can be seen. Slumber had overpowered me and robbed me of any sightseeing, but I felt refreshed because of it.

As the station platform came closer, I could see a man and a woman standing on the dock. They stood out from the crowd and, judging by the way they were dressed, clearly looked American. I thought that they must certainly be the Schellings, and I was somewhat embarrassed to meet them for the first time wearing my unkempt French military uniform, which was in tatters.

My embarrassment was short-lived, however, as I was to learn that the news of my capture and escape had spread quickly and was already the subject of speculative newspaper stories—my tattered uniform, proof of my ordeal, was now a badge of courage and honor.

As I stepped out of the passenger car onto the platform I could hear someone calling my name. "Tommy, Tommy Hitchcock! Ernest and Lucie Schelling here!" I quickly approached and introduced myself.

"Welcome to Berne, Tommy. We exchanged cables with your father and mother in Aiken once we confirmed that you had boarded the train in Thayngen, and assured them that you are now safe, and welcome to stay with us as long as you wish," said Ernest.

"Thank you, Mr. Schelling, I appreciate your hospitality, but I plan to get back to Paris as soon as possible and learn what my status is at this point and hopefully re-join my comrades at the front. But, before

---

56   To be "breveted" is a French military ceremony where pilots receive their flying insignias and are recognized as having met the standards of military aviation training.

that I need to sit down and write *Maman* as I promised I would," said I.

"Certainly, Tommy, take whatever time you need," said Schelling as he led the way down the platform and headed to where his auto was parked.

"You'll have our son's room since he's now in the States. It has all the quiet privacy you may want," he added.

The Schellings owned an elegant villa in the mountains about a fifteen-minute ride from the train station. There Tommy would stay for three days during which he rested, arranged his transportation to Paris, and wrote his letter as promised to his mother, who was already at their Aiken home for the season:

September 1918

Dear Maman,

So much has happened since we last saw one another, and I don't know where to begin this letter, but first know that I am safe and well here in Berne, and I miss you and Papa very dearly.

Perhaps it makes sense to begin by bringing you up to date concerning the events that have taken place since my last sortie near the French-German border:

On March 6th two other pilots, French Captains Agire, d'Estainville, and myself, were on routine patrol from our base in Luneville, about ten kilometers from the German border. We were flying in formation, when over Nancy, we came across two German Albatrosses; targets too tempting to ignore. We had been trained to defend French airspace first, and as such, my comrades turned to remain over French territory. I broke formation, gunned the engine into a climb, and went for the two who were now heading toward and proceeding to cross the German border. With two kills to my credit, I saw this as an opportunity to come closer to my goal of becoming an "Ace." In retrospect I may have not used the best judgment, but at the time it made perfect sense.

The two Albatrosses were now below me, circling, and as I began my descent to attack, and before I could open fire on the two in my gun sight, I heard and felt machine gun fire coming from my rear. Unbeknown to me a third German fighter had been in the clouds behind me, and now he was in my rear tearing up my plane with machine gun fire. I could not get into position to return fire, so I turned to head back to the French border trying to evade his shots and hoping he would back off, but he did not, and with my rudder knocked out, bullet holes in my wings, and a wound in my buttocks and thigh I went down—in German territory.

The next thing I remember was being carried by German soldiers to a prisoner of war hospital where I remained for several weeks. In April I was moved to another prison hospital in Saarbrucken that I shared with some Russian POWs. On May 1st I was again transferred, although this move was to a prison camp, not a hospital. I knew it was time to begin planning my escape.

The German POW camp I was taken to was located in Giessen where I was processed and sent on to Darmstadt where I was to be assigned a "permanent" prison camp. On May 15th we were placed aboard a troop train and began heading east to a town called Landshut, where we were temporarily housed in a thirteenth century castle-turned- prison, called Trousnitz Castle. There, I met up with other American and British prisoners of war who were also bent on escaping. My comrades and I discussed a number of escape plans, but before we could activate any plan, I, along with a couple of other Americans, was moved again. This time to a POW camp specifically for Americans, and it was during that particular train ride that I made my escape.

I have been told that the story of my crash and escape is being recounted in the U.S. newspapers portraying me as some sort of hero. I don't think of it that way, and I am somewhat embarrassed at being captured. It never should have happened, and I am trying to put it all behind me and return to my unit.

I will be leaving here in a couple of days for Paris to report in and request reassignment to my unit, wherever they may now be. I will be sure to contact you from Paris, and until then I remain,

Your Loving Son,
Tommy

THE REST OF THE STORY

Thomas & Louise Hitchcock were very upset by their son's daring adventures in the war, and feared for his safety. They were not without influence in the upper regions of the federal government, and felt that he would be safer in the United States Army Air Corps. To this end, and without Tommy's knowledge, they exerted their influence, and his "transfer" paperwork to the U.S. Army Air Corps began to process. When Tommy arrived in Paris and contacted his French military superiors, he was told that his status was in limbo because of high-ranking orders from Washington, and as such, he could not be reassigned. As he stewed in Paris for a while, he did not know which country's air corps he belonged to. The U.S. had put a hold on him for military service, despite the fact that it was his desire to continue the fight there and remain a part of the French military, particularly since the French had awarded him a promotion to *sous-lieutenant* for his heroic action. His frustrated efforts to be reassigned to his old French air unit went on for two months, ending on November 11, 1918, when the war came to an end. He was angry with his parents for interfering with his plans to remain in France's military and told them so in a terse letter sent just prior to the war's end. Immediately following the armistice, he boarded a ship and sailed back home to Old Westbury, New York.

Tommy Hitchcock, Jr. was a very extraordinary individual throughout his short life. Following the war, Tommy bent to parental pressure and entered Harvard College. In his first summer break of 1919, he returned to his favorite sport, polo, and was on his way to becoming the most renowned player in America and, as many thought, the world. His on-field prowess was directly influenced by his air combat experience: speed and aggressive tactics designed to stymie the foe, combined with a hand-eye precision very few in the sport could match. For Tommy, the game of polo was an extension of, and in a sense a peacetime substitute for, air combat. He played during his time at Harvard, where his academic focus, chemical engineering, took a backseat to polo; his nature was action, not academics.

As his polo fame spread, and was combined with tales of his heroic wartime experiences, he acquired many friends and admirers throughout the country and overseas, including certain Hollywood celebrities, such as Will Rogers. His Hollywood connections were facilitated by the fact that polo was spreading rapidly in California, where some of the most skilled and aggressive players in the country were emerging, and where Tommy competed from time to time.

F. Scott Fitzgerald so admired Hitchcock that he based two of his main characters in his novels, *The Great Gatsby* and *Tender Is the Night*, after him. We know this from Fitzgerald's own statements. Hitchcock possessed all the heroic and manly qualities that Fitzgerald lacked. And Fitzgerald was not alone, as there were others from the polo, business, political, and theatrical world who shared that admiration—two of whom would play a role in Tommy's future.

One writer called the '20s and '30s the Tommy Hitchcock years in polo, just as there were Babe Ruth years in baseball, and Bobby Jones years in golf. Throughout the 1920s and 1930s, Hitchcock, who carried a ten-goal handicap, the highest ranking in polo, led four teams to the U.S. National Open Polo Championship: 1923, 1927, 1935, and 1936. Throughout the years he played with, and against, some of the best polo players in the world. Variously, he played alongside such notables who were also Aiken winter visitors: Pete Bostwick, Devereux

Millburn, Harry Payne Whitney, Jock Whitney, Gerald Balding, and Averill Harriman, among others.

Tommy was a member of the Meadow Brook Club in Westbury, New York. Meadow Brook was the established polo Mecca of the East. Its white, Anglo-Saxon, Christian membership came from the upper ranks of society, as polo was a gentleman's sport in the East.[57] Jews were not allowed membership at Meadow Brook. In response to this, a Jewish businessman and polo player named Julius Fleischmann[58] began the Sand Point Club in Long Island primarily for Jews, but it was open to anyone who wanted to play polo. A prominent member there who was to figure in Tommy's future was Robert Lehman. Tommy was also a member of the Sand Point Club, and became friends with Lehman.

In the fall of 1927, Tommy was introduced to a young widow by the name of Peggy Mellon Laughlin during lunch at the Plaza Hotel in New York. Ms. Laughlin was the daughter of William Larimer Mellon, Sr., who was a founder of the Gulf Oil Corporation in 1907, later to become one of the largest oil companies in the U.S.

On December 15th 1928, after a year of courtship, Tommy Hitchcock and Peggy Mellon Laughlin were married in a modest ceremony that took place on neutral[59] ground, the Plaza Hotel in New York City.[60] Following the wedding the couple left on a two-week honeymoon to Hawaii.

In 1937, Tommy's polo pal from Sand Point Club, Robert Lehman, offered him a partnership with his company, Lehman Brothers, an

---

57   Polo caught on rapidly in Texas, where it was practiced in a wild and wooly fashion, as spurred cowboys on western saddles played on open pastures.
58   Fleischmann began the Fleischmann Yeast Company and later (following prohibition) began a successful liquor business. He was a frequent winter visitor to Aiken, and his name can be found in Aiken's New Highland Park Hotel register, where he regularly stayed.
59   Hitchcock was a Catholic and the Mellons were devout Presbyterians.
60   Tommy was working on Wall Street as a bond trader at that time, making New York a convenient city in which to be married.

investment banking firm co-founded by Robert's grandfather, Emanuel Lehman, in 1850. Upon receiving the offer, Tommy protested that he didn't know anything about investment banking, to which Lehman gave his oft repeated motto, "I believe in people." Of course, Lehman also knew Hitchcock's character, forthrightness, and honesty, and had played polo with him on numerous occasions. Tommy accepted the position.

Like many other patriotic Americans, the outbreak of World War II stirred Tommy's desire for action, as it had for World War I. However, by this time Tommy was forty-one years old and ineligible for military service due to his age. His strong desire to return to duty as a military pilot (this time in the U.S. Army Air Corps) and take part in the war as he did during WWI would not be frustrated due to his age. His opportunity came when a chance meeting occurred with a former teacher from St. Paul's School, Gil Winant,[61] who had also flown in WWI and who now was the American ambassador to England. Winant remembered Tommy from the St. Paul's days, had been following his high-profile polo victories reported in the national press, and was very aware of his experiences in France's Lafayette Flying Corps. Tommy indicated his interest in getting into the war, and as the conversation went, Winant asked him to submit a letter to him requesting assignment to the U.S. Embassy in London, citing his past military aviation experience. This done, Winant requested a position be created—Assistant U.S. Military Attaché—as a liaison between the Eighth Air Force and the RAF's Fighter Command, and recommended Tommy Hitchcock for the job.

When Tommy arrived in London in 1942, bombers, not fighter aircraft, dominated allied air activity and took center stage in the air war. The general command believed that knocking out the enemy's material support resources through bombing was the way to end the war.

---

61   See Lynne Olson's well-researched book, *Citizens of London*, pub. 2010 by Random House, for detailed information about Winant and Hitchcock's relationship and role in WWII London.

Unfortunately, bombers became easy targets for German fighter pilots, who wreaked havoc, taking a heavy toll on unprotected bombers during missions. Tommy believed that fighter aircraft were necessary to protect bombing convoys and ultimately, after many bomber shoot downs (and many letters and meetings), he was able to exert his view on military strategy and became involved in the development of the P-51 Mustang, a fighter airplane that was to have a major impact on turning the tide in the air war. The Mustang was initially being built in the U.S. by North American Aviation Company for the RAF, and this is how Tommy became acquainted with it.

By 1944, Tommy Hitchcock's tenacity paid off and the P-51 was adopted as the U.S. Army Air Corps' fighter of choice. As a result, he was given new duties in fighter aircraft research and development. His true desire would have been to fly a Mustang into battle, but this he would be denied. He is credited with the statement, "Fighting in a Mustang ought to be like playing polo—but with pistols."

On April 19, 1944, he drove out to Salisbury, an airfield located outside of London. Although he had test pilots at his disposal, he decided to personally take up a test Mustang on this particular day. He took the aircraft up to fifteen thousand feet, flew it over a bombing range, and placed the aircraft into a dive—a dive from which it would never emerge. Tommy Hitchcock died on that day at the age of forty-four, a result of a test aircraft crash.

It was left to Gil Winant, U.S. Ambassador to Great Britain, to notify his wife of his tragic death.

He was buried in the Cambridge American Cemetery, Cambridgeshire, England.

THE REMARKABLE ISELINS

October 13, 1893

On Friday morning, the ocean off the coast of Sandy Hook, New Jersey, was beginning to turn mean. The sun was in a futile death struggle with a graying autumn sky. The moderating breeze of yesterday had picked up speed, and the usual easy swells were developing a green-gray chop. Ribbons of dislodged brown and green kelp could be seen swaying in the troughs between the white-tipped rollers.

A hurricane was on its way to the North Carolina/South Carolina border, and taking aim at central Pennsylvania. The outermost bands of the storm were nibbling at the edges of the mid-Atlantic states, but for now it didn't matter. It didn't matter because, if things went well today, the racing yacht *Vigilant*,[62] owned by a syndicate[63] led by C. Oliver Iselin of New Rochelle, NY and Aiken, SC, would take the best out of five races, repulse the British challenger again, and for the ninth time, earn the right to retain America's Cup in what many thought was its rightful place—within the walls of the New York Yacht Club.

Vigilant's British challenger on this day was *Valkyrie II*[64] owned by Windham Wyndham-Quin, the 4th Earl of Dunraven. Dunraven had previously challenged for the Cup in 1889 with *Valkyrie*, but was disqualified for a rules violation en route to the dock in New York. But, he was back today and would need to win all three remaining races in the best out of five series in order to take the Cup back to Britain.

---

62 *Vigilant* was a 124-foot centerboard racing sloop with a displacement of 138 tons, designed and built by Herreshoff Manufacturing Co. of Bristol, Rhode Island. Cost to build in 1893 was $100,000 (equivalent to $2,400,000 today).

63 Iselin was the syndicate's managing partner with his father, Adrian Iselin, August Belmont, Jr., Cornelius Vanderbilt, Charles R. Flint, Chester W. Chapin, George R. Clark, Henry Astor Carey, Dr. Barton Hopkins, E.M. Fulton, Jr., and Edward D. Morgan. They were all members of the New York Yacht Club.

64 *Valkyrie II* was a 117-foot gaff-rigged cutter with a displacement of 140 tons. It was designed by George Lenox Watson, and built by D&W Henderson for the Earl of Dunraven.

Losing today would mean a close-out for the English and a sweep for the Americans.

What was especially significant about this America's Cup defense was that the helmsman would be the sloop's designer and builder, Nathanael Greene Herreshoff.

In 1790, Herreshoff's grandfather Frederick emigrated to Bristol, Rhode Island, from Prussia, where he had been a boat builder. Nathanael was one of nine children born to Frederick Herreshoff, Jr. on March 18, 1848, and built his first boat, *The Tadpole*, at the age of ten. As a young man he was a student at Massachusetts Institute of Technology, where from 1866 to 1869, he mastered the engineering theories that would later help to pave his way to becoming the leading nautical designer of his time, and some say, of all time. He and his blind brother, John Brown Herreshoff, operated the Herreshoff Manufacturing Company in Bristol, and were responsible for designing and building racing yachts for America's Cup defense from 1893 to 1920.

It was unusual that a yacht's designer/builder would also serve as captain. However, Iselin asked "Captain Nat" if he would take the helm for the 1893 series as he felt *Vigilant's* most advanced design, testing the limits of nautical engineering, could best be handled by its creator. This pivotal race in the series would cover fifteen miles windward from Scotland Lighthouse off Sandy Hook, and the return leeward to the starting point. As managing partner, C. Oliver Iselin had total control over nearly every aspect of *Vigilant's* defense of the Cup, from design, construction, and launch, to race strategy and crew selection.

C. Oliver Iselin was born in New York in 1854. He was the son of Adrian Iselin, whose father came to the U.S. in the early 1800s from Basel, Switzerland, where he was a capitalist in the silk and glove trade. C. Oliver's father was the founder of the banking house A. Iselin & Company located on Wall Street in New York City. At the outbreak of the War between the States, C. Oliver's father had already amassed a fortune and became a lender to the U.S. government. The family's wealth was further expanded with investments in railroad, mining, and real estate. His mother was the former Miss Eleanora O'Donnell, a devout Catholic and a substantial benefactor to the Catholic Church. The family made their home in New Rochelle, New York, on the Long Island Sound, where C. Oliver learned to sail at a very young age.

While still in his teens, C. Oliver received lessons in sailboat racing from the family's boatman, and began to develop a reputation as a racing master. In 1874, he graduated from Columbia Law School and began working at his father's bank. Sports, especially sailing, were the greater passions that drew him from the working world to the world of competitive sailing. At the age of twenty-three, he was elected to the New York Yacht Club, where his reputation as a yachtsman continued to grow, and in 1887, he served as a crewmember aboard the racing yacht *Volunteer*[65] in its successful defense of America's Cup. There is no doubt that Iselin's success aboard *Volunteer* contributed to his accession to managing partner in the building and sailing of *Vigilant* in this latest defense of the Cup. By this time C. Oliver was considered to be the best amateur yachtsman in the country.

In 1893 Iselin was a widower. His wife, the former Frances "Fannie" Garner, had passed away in 1890.[66] Four children issued from the marriage: Eleanora Iselin, Fannie Garner Iselin, Adrian Iselin, and Charles Oliver Iselin, Jr. No doubt they continued to occupy his thoughts, but at this moment, his thoughts and energy were focused on defeating *Valkyrie II* at all cost. The British had never won, and he was determined that they never would win while on his watch.

As the *Vigilant* and the *Valkyrie II* were being towed from their slips in New York Harbor to the starting point, the wind speed continued to increase. Now all spectator eyes were trained on the sleek design of the giant yacht conjured by the "Wizard of Bristol," Nathanael Herreshoff, as it silently moved among the white-capped waves.

Three statuesque men stood out on *Vigilant's* deck as the yacht began to make its way into the harbor. The bearded Herreshoff, with weathered hand on helm, staring a seaman's gaze and radiating a palpable

---

65   *Volunteer* defeated the yacht *Thistle* 2-0. *Thistle* was sponsored by the Royal Clyde Yacht Club of Great Britain.

66   Alternative sources give Frances Garner Iselin's death as 1892.

confidence inherited from his Teutonic forebears. By his side stood the hawk-eyed C. Oliver Iselin in seaman's cap, directing the crew to their duties of making initial preparations to sails and boom. The other men standing on deck were Edward Dennison Morgan, syndicate partner, and Herbert C. Leeds, who would be serving as navigator for the race.

The wind had increased to nearly gale force[67] as the yachts were approaching the Scotland Lightship, starting point for the race. Upwards of sixty thousand witnesses—on land, in spectator boats, and on steamers and pleasure boats—were watching and anxiously awaiting the starter's cannon with high hopes for another American victory.

As the two yachts drew near to the starting line, the starter's ball dropped and the cannon boom sounded.

Immediately *Valkyrie II* leaped across the line and darted ahead of *Vigilant* to establish a lead that would widen as the English yacht continued down the windward leg.

Because of the increasingly forceful winds, Captain Nat ordered *Vigilant's* sails reefed,[68] lest risk the possibility that they be torn to shreds. *Valkyrie II* had already done the same.

With every rise and fall of their bows, the two yachts kicked up spray as they plowed through an agitated, foam-blown sea. Crewmembers were doused as they lay prone upon the deck lest they create wind resistance. With her rail even with the ocean's chop, *Vigilant* radically heeled,[69] and only her thirteen-foot leaded center board was preventing her from capsizing. All canvas was stretched to the maximum, tautness testing the strength of her towering mast.

The challenger from Britain continued to outpace the defending Americans as the halfway mark came into sight. The English rounded the halfway point two minutes ahead of *Vigilant* in one of the fastest runs in America's Cup history. Seeing *Valkyrie's* stern round the half turn, an anxious Captain Nat tightened his grip on the helm. His wrinkled brow and set jaw reflected the intensity of the situation that was

---

67   Near gale force is characterized by 28- to 33-knot winds with 13- to 19-foot waves.
68   Reefing is done to reduce the size of a sail by partially lowering it and binding the excess cloth in stops.
69   To heel is to lean or tilt on edge due to the force wind exerts on the sails.

rapidly escalating. His eyes flashed as he turned to Iselin with a knowing look, and without a word being said, both men knew what needed to be done to have a fighting chance as they approached the mid-race turn.

"Release the reef on mainsail, set the spinnaker, and balloon jib topsail, and topsail," growled Herreshoff, sending scrambling crewmembers across the salt-washed deck, through the wind-flung spray. With his order, every square foot of *Vigilant's* sails was released against the driving high wind. The die was cast, the gamble made, and his hope was that the straining mast and every piece of cloth would hold against the ever-increasing gale force. *Vigilant*, responding to the added sail, began to leap through the foam and with each second make strides, closing the gap on the English. Seeing *Vigilant* now almost abreast of their yacht, the crew of *Valkyrie II* did likewise, releasing every bit of cloth available in an attempt to maintain their lead.

Both vessels were now abreast, dangerously close, so close that the crew on the heeling *Valiant's* deck were looking up at *Valkyrie's* towering, exposed keel, and leaving little room for error. The violent wind was now at gale speed, washing inclined decks on each downward plunge, followed by blowing foam high into the gleaming wet sails with each upward thrust. Crewmen frantically clung to whatever they could, unable to see for the blowing saltwater flying into their faces. Despite the storm-like conditions, Herreshoff and Iselin, like concrete fixtures, stood firmly at the helm guiding the yacht with deft precision, taking full advantage of the wind filling *Vigilant's* fully set sails.

Then it happened!

With a thunderously loud rip and whap, *Valkyrie II's* two spinnakers,[70] unable to withstand the wind force, ripped apart and in tatters began to flap helplessly against their stays. Without her spinnakers, *Valkyrie II* could not maintain the speed necessary to win. She began to fall back, and her hapless crew could do nothing but watch as *Valiant* surged ahead to the finish line.

---

70   The spinnaker is a large parachute-like three-sided sail set forward of the mast and used when sailing downwind.

Valiant crossed the finish forty seconds[71] ahead of *Valkyrie II*, sweeping the series and winning the right to retain the America's Cup. The collective sigh of relief was quickly replaced by jubilation as Herreshoff, Iselin, Leeds, and Morgan extended hearty congratulations to their crew.

As *Valiant* was towed back into New York Harbor, it was met by euphoric, adoring crowds on docks, pleasure boats, sightseeing vessels, and a sea of waving white handkerchiefs accompanied by shouts of approval and pride in what they had just witnessed. Military ships fired their cannons; marine fire control boats trained their hoses on the sky, creating cascades of water in a nautical salute. It was a glorious day for the United States and C. Oliver Iselin.

Not long after his Cup victory, Iselin began showing "marked attention," as one newspaper noted, toward Miss Hope Goddard of Providence, Rhode Island. The attraction must have been strong and mutual, since their engagement was announced on May 5, 1894, with the wedding following one month later, in a simple ceremony at the bride's father's home. The service was performed by Rev. C. A. L. Richards, rector of St. John's Episcopal Church, Providence, Rhode Island.

Hope Goddard[72] was born on January 17, 1868 to Colonel William Goddard and Mary Edith Jenckes Goddard of Providence, Rhode Island. At the outbreak of the War Between the States, Hope's father became a volunteer and was commissioned a colonel of the First Light Infantry of Rhode Island. He distinguished himself at the battle of Bull Run, and later became aide-de-camp to General Burnside. Following the war he returned to Rhode Island and became engaged in industry,

---

71   *Valiant* actually won by a significantly higher margin, but due to the yacht's handicap as a favorite to win, forty seconds reflected its official time with handicap applied.
72   Née Edith Hope Goddard.

and was later elected chancellor of Brown University in 1888.

Hope was a member of the wealthy and prominent Rhode Island family descended from Moses Brown Ives Goddard. Beginning in the newspaper business, the Goddard family later established a management company, Goddard Brothers Agents, in 1850, which managed the Lonsdale and Hope companies, part of a prosperous textile and manufacturing business. Additionally, they owned large blocks of government bonds, stocks in leading railroad companies, electric, gas, insurance, and banking companies as well. As a young girl, Hope was introduced to northeastern society and spent summers visiting Newport, Europe, and New York.

Although the Goddard family maintained homes in Providence and Potowamut, an exclusive enclave near East Greenwich, Rhode Island, they did visit Aiken during winters of the late 1800s. It was reported that young Hope experienced breathing difficulty[73] and the trips were for health purposes. During those winters the Goddard family would lease Aiken cottages, and reportedly leased the well-known Rye Patch Cottage on at least one occasion.

As a girl, Hope gained a love of sports, including golf and equine, particularly thoroughbreds, and in later years established racing stables at her estate in Upper Brookville, Long Island, and in England. Her interest in equestrian activities brought her closer to the Whitneys and Hitchcocks, family friends who shared that interest.

Hope was William Goddard's only daughter, and she along with her mother stood to inherit vast wealth upon her father's death.[74]

As Aiken's reputation as an equestrian center grew among the nation's elite, Hope and Oliver established a winter home there called Hopelands, so named after the only surviving child[75] of their marriage, where Hope maintained stables for the sport she most dearly loved. It was only after her marriage to Iselin that she acquired a love for yacht

---

73   Similar physical difficulty to befall Louise Eustis Hitchcock.

74   William Goddard died in 1907.

75   In September 1909, Hope and Oliver Iselin's firstborn, William Iselin, seven years of age, died at Baden-Baden, Germany. A daughter, Hope, was the second child born to them.

racing, and became the first American[76] woman to crew on a vessel defending America's Cup.

May 16, 1917
Hopelands
Aiken, South Carolina

Hopelands was a beautiful fifteen-acre estate, and on this sparkling spring morning in Aiken, its splendid white cottage, accented by its green-striped awning windows, stood out in full glory. The property was a wedding gift[77] from Colonel William Goddard to his daughter and son-in-law. He had purchased the land from Frank L. Burckhalter and Elizabeth B. Bates in March of 1897 for $1,650. Around the turn of the century, the Iselins commissioned the New York architectural firm of Hoppin and Koen to design their home, the same firm that designed their summer home, Wolver Hollow, in Upper Brooksville, Long Island.

Hope Iselin was a lady of varied interests. She loved her thoroughbreds, her dogs, and beautifying her property with cedars, live oaks, azaleas, dogwoods, and various other plants. Perhaps a trait she inherited from her father, she also felt a sense of responsibility to her community. In Rhode Island, the Goddards had donated property for use by Brown University, in addition to land given to the city of Providence for parks and recreational use. Goddard Park is well known to Rhode Islanders. Likewise, the Iselin family had been generous to the Catholic Church and City of New Rochelle, New York. Her civic interest as well as Oliver's was evident, as they both took part in a number of Aiken's organizations, including The Aiken Hospital and Relief Society, an organization upon which the couple was making a significant imprint.

Like on many other spring mornings, this morning she was busy working in her garden, checking the progress of past plantings and

---

76   Hope crewed on racing yacht *Columbia* in the 1899 race. The first woman to crew on an America's Cup challenge was British—Lord Dunraven's daughter in the 1893 race won by Iselin's *Vigilant*.

77   Although it was considered a wedding gift, the property was purchased three years after the marriage.

making last additions before returning to the north for the summer. As she worked, her thoughts were on their little daughter, Hope, on whom she and Oliver doted. As a little girl, Hope spent much of her time playing on the estate with the family pets and in the large dollhouse her parents had bought for her through the Sears and Roebuck catalogue. Education was important to the Iselins. A tutor was employed through the winter, and classes took place in Hope's dollhouse. It would appear that the Iselins were overprotective of their daughter, as they kept her close since the death of their seven-year-old son William, following an illness while visiting Baden-Baden, Germany, in 1909.

Mrs. Iselin had other things on her mind this morning; the dinner party she was hosting this evening at the Willcox Hotel, and the reception on the morrow, dedicating the new Aiken Hospital. She and Oliver, along with a number of other winter colonists, generously gave of their time and money to build Aiken's first hospital on land donated by the city at Eustis Park.[78] She had provided a list of her dinner guests to Frederick Willcox at the hotel, and it included a select group of other wealthy northern couples who would also serve on the new hospital's board of directors: Colonel Anthony Kuser, William K. Vanderbilt, Mrs. Clarence Dolan, Mrs. Thomas Hitchcock, Jr., and Mrs. Sheffield Phelps. She also invited Aiken's mayor, W. J. Moseley, who would represent the local members[79] of the new hospital's board. The mayor would also be presiding at tomorrow's dedication ceremony.

There was one other special dinner guest who would be present at the Willcox this evening—Captain Nathanael Herreshoff. Oliver hadn't seen his old friend and yachting comrade for some time. Although Captain Nat was still building racing yachts for America's Cup defense,[80] Oliver had had his last Cup defense in 1903[81] aboard

---

78   The land given by the city had been donated to the city by Celestine Eustis for use as a public park.

79   Local board members included Mr. J. Salley, Mrs. H. H. Wyman, Mrs. W. W. Muckenfuss, Mr. H. M. Dibble, Mrs. D. S. Henderson, Mrs. Daniel Crossland, Mrs. H. V. Wyman, and Dr. H. J. Ray.

80   Herreshoff built his last America's Cup yacht in 1920.

81   Iselin successfully defended America's Cup on six occasions: 1887, 1893, 1895, 1899, 1901, 1903.

the racing yacht *Reliance*. Herreshoff had begun spending winters in Palm Beach, and was making his spring return to Rhode Island, taking time for a side trip to Aiken to visit the Iselins. His train would be coming into the Aiken Depot this afternoon.

"Hope, Hope, where are you?" She could hear her husband's familiar voice coming from the far entrance of the home.

"Oliver, I'm here in the garden," she replied without turning from her work of fastidiously trimming an overgrown azalea.

"Darling, I'm off to Palmetto for a round of golf with Herbert and Thomas,[82] and I will be home in time to collect Captain Nat at the station," he said as he hoisted his clubs over his shoulder for the short walk to the Palmetto Golf Club.

The first four holes of the Palmetto Golf Club were created by William C. Whitney and Thomas Hitchcock in 1892. In 1895, five holes were added, and Herbert Leeds, Aiken winter colonist and designer of the Myopia Hunt Club Golf Course in the Boston area, helped to redesign the nine-hole tract. Around 1897, William C. Whitney purchased and donated additional land abutting the club, and the course was expanded to eighteen holes. By 1917, its membership roster was virtually a who's who of American elite, a trend that would continue for many years.

Oliver had not yet shared his plans for today's golf match with his wife. He and his golf partners' usual wager was one hundred dollars[83] per player, but today he would propose doubling that amount. Should he win, he had already decided to donate the funds to the Aiken Hospital Relief Society. Should he lose, he would propose that the winner make the donation.

The Iselins led the group of winter colonists who built the hospital at a cost of forty-four thousand dollars.[84] Additionally, they accounted for some of the equipment, along with certain local citizens and businesses that pledged to help outfit the building. He knew that more was

---

82   Both Herbert Leeds and Thomas Hitchcock served with Iselin on the Palmetto Golf Club's Board of Governors in 1902 and later.

83    $200 in 1917 would equal approximately $3,600 today.

84    $44,000 in 1917 would equal approximately $790,000 today.

needed to improve on the furnishings, including an additional X-ray machine, and this was the motivation for doubling the wager for today's golf match.

Taking a late lunch, Captain Nat sat in the dining car of the Southern Railway train, which was clattering through Georgia and would soon be arriving at the Aiken Train Depot. He was now sixty-nine years of age and because of the Great War now raging in Europe, there were no challengers for America's Cup, and therefore no expensive, leviathan sailing yachts to be built. Because of his reputation with the New York Yacht Club, he continued to build personal sail and power boats for wealthy members there, but the impact of the War had caused the Herreshoff Manufacturing Company's fortunes to decline. He now quietly contemplated the future of his company.[85] His health was becoming an issue as well, which was the reason for his perennial winter stays in Florida, as the harsh Rhode Island winters had become more stressful for him.

Herreshoff's thoughts now turned to his friend Oliver Iselin. There would be so much news to exchange, as it had been since 1903 that he had last collaborated with Oliver on a Cup yacht, and the two had kept only sporadic correspondence.

As Herreshoff's train was arriving to a waiting Oliver at the Aiken depot, Hope Iselin had gone to meet with Frederick Willcox to review details for this evening's soirée.

"Mr. Willcox, I know you probably have everything in order, but I would like to go over the guest list and tonight's menu with you one more time, to be sure everything is as it should be," she said as she sat with Frederick in his private office.

"Why certainly, Mrs. Iselin, I've prepared this list for you in advance so you could re-check and approve tonight's menu and other details that we've previously discussed," said Frederick, in his usual accommodating manner.

As she studied Frederick's list she said, "All appears to be in order.

---

85   He built his last racing yacht for the Cup's defense in 1920. *Resolute* defeated Sir Thomas Lipton's *Shamrock IV*.

Guests will begin arriving about seven for cocktails. Would you please have at least two barmen on hand, and with dinner we will want the 1910 Bordeaux, if it is still available. I know the war in Europe has affected supply of the better wines," she added as she approached the hotel foyer to leave, "but I know you will do your best."

"Certainly, Mrs. Iselin, we look forward to seeing you this evening," replied Frederick.

Captain Nat and Oliver were now ensconced, with snifters of cognac, in Hopelands' well-appointed living room, exchanging memories of times past, when Hope arrived home.

"Captain Nat, what a pleasure to see you! It has been so long. I hope you have been well," she said as she noticed, without giving evidence of her dismay, how the old captain had aged since their last meeting.

"Yes, it has been a long time, Hope, and I trust you have been well for these past years," he said as he rose to embrace her. "Oliver and I were just remembering the Cup race of 1903, and the bloody fog that was so thick we couldn't see Lipton's[86] boat, and only using our instruments for guidance were we able to know where the finish line was. You were the best onboard timekeeper, haven't had one as good since then, Hope," he added with fond reflection.

"Thank you, Captain Nat, I always treasure your compliments. Now, has Oliver told you about our new hospital that we are dedicating tomorrow?" she asked as Oliver handed her a glass of red Bordeaux, her favorite.

"He has told me a bit about it. I understand many of the individuals responsible for its building will be present at the dinner you are hosting. I appreciate your invitation to take part this evening. I understand that the official dedication will take place tomorrow, and that you and Oliver will be making the presentation," he said.

"Yes, that's right. But, you know, a very dangerous situation has

---

86   Sir Thomas Lipton of grocery and tea company fame challenged with his *Shamrock III* in 1903. Coming from a common birth, he was raised to the peerage by the queen, but was still derisively referred to as "The Grocer" by hereditary nobility.

persisted here with Aiken being without its own hospital. We realized just how many lives could be saved by having a hospital nearby, and the Aiken Hospital and Relief Society was formed not very long ago. Tomorrow's dedication represents the culmination of our efforts," she explained.

"Tell me a little about the building, Hope," Herreshoff asked.

She took a sip of her wine and began.

"Well, the building consists of a basement and three floors. The basement holds the power plant, with the most modern boiler for hot and cold water, and a protective plant against fire. The morgue and autopsy room are also located there. The first floor is designed for patient intake and has two reception rooms; one for colored, and one for white. Sitting rooms for nurses, the kitchen and dining room, and four bedrooms are also located there. The second floor contains the operating room, five private rooms, the hospital surgeon's quarters, the X-ray studio, nurses' work room, a storage area for bandages and medicines, and sterilizing room. The third floor consists of the superintendant's suite, and is connected to the west wing of rooms. We have a total of thirty rooms for patients, which hopefully will be adequate for a while. We have also guaranteed the maintenance expense for the next five years," she added.

Glancing at the stately clock in Hopelands' hall, Mrs. Iselin turned to the men and said, "The time is getting late, gentlemen, and we should be readying ourselves for dinner."

But before anyone could rise, Oliver interjected, "I have an announcement to make that will be made public at dinner this evening by our dear friend Thomas Hitchcock. This afternoon at our golf match, I proposed a wager of two hundred per man, and both Herbert and Thomas agreed, once I explained my purpose. I told them that, should I win the match, I plan to donate the winnings for an additional X-ray machine for the hospital. Well, I lost, and Leeds should have won because he is the superior golfer, but Thomas won. Not to be outdone, he plans to give his winnings to the Hospital Relief Fund. I expect Mayor Moseley will want to make the announcement at tomorrow's dedication, but I don't expect Thomas wants any publicity from it. I believe it will be made with anonymity," he said.

"What a wonderful surprise, darling," Hope exclaimed. "And I'm sure Thomas will want to remain anonymous, just as Mr. Vanderbilt did when I gave my poker winnings from him to the cause. Now, let us repair to the dressing rooms, lest we be late in welcoming our guests at the Willcox…"

THE REST OF THE STORY

The Aiken Hospital's official name was Aiken Hospital and Relief Society and did in fact open on May 17, 1917 following a dedication ceremony. It was constructed by a local African-American-owned construction firm, McGhee and McGhee. Its cost of $44,900 to build was borne almost exclusively by winter colony residents who, in addition to providing the building cost, guaranteed its maintenance expenses for the five years following its founding. That effort was spearheaded by C. Oliver and Hope Iselin. In 1924, the hospital was forced to close due to a lack of funds. In 1927, Aiken County government leased the property and reopened the facility in June of that year. In 1936, a new Aiken County Hospital was constructed on the site, replacing the original building.

C. Oliver Iselin was first and foremost a yachtsman. His active involvement in the building, management, and sailing in defense of America's Cup from 1887 to 1903 is legendary to this very day. Iselin was very patriotic and considered his role in the Cup races against British challengers to not only be competitive, but one of national pride where failure was not an option. He never lost an America's Cup race.

His first marriage to Francis (Fannie) Garner ended with her death in 1892. There were four children from that marriage: Elenora Iselin, who was later to become a countess through her marriage to Count Ferdinand Colloredo-Mansfield of Austria; Fannie Garner Iselin, who was born in Paris; Adrian Iselin, who was named for his paternal grandfather; and Charles Oliver Iselin, Jr.

In 1894, at age forty he married Hope Goddard and was introduced to Aiken, as Hope had visited there with her parents in earlier years. Two children came from the marriage: a son, William (1902), and a daughter, Hope (1907).

An intense individual, Iselin's health began to falter in 1905 when he suffered a nervous breakdown. Although he made a full recovery, it was reported that his condition was aggravated by the death of his father in that same year. In September 1909, he suffered a family tragedy when his seven-year-old son William died while visiting Baden-Baden, Germany, a city that C. Oliver visited many times. William had been the only male child issuing from his marriage with Hope Goddard, and the loss was particularly tragic.

Iselin died on January 1, 1932 at his New York home, Wolver Hollow, at Glen Head, Long Island. In his will he bequeathed a generous financial gift to Aiken's Schofield Industrial School. Additionally, as a memorial to his deceased son William, he provided $50,000 in trust for the Aiken Hospital and Relief Society. Even in death he continued his commitment to Aiken's hospital, which he and Hope worked so diligently to create.

Hope Goddard Iselin was twenty-six years old when she married C. Oliver Iselin. It was her first marriage. Coming from the wealthy Goddard family of Rhode Island, she would eventually become a prominent social leader, rivaling one of her dear friends, Louise Hitchcock. Like Mrs. Hitchcock, she eschewed conventionality and violated contemporary rules for women by being the first American woman to crew on an America's Cup racing yacht, which drew the ire of the Daughters of the American Revolution. She was an accomplished golfer who had the audacity to challenge and defeat the Russian Grand Duke Michael, at a famous tournament sponsored by the duke of Wales in 1900. She was graceful and accepted her win with a smile, while the grand duke smashed his clubs in a rage over having been defeated by a woman.

She was a horsewoman of the first rank, maintaining stables in Aiken, New York, and England. She loved her dogs and raising Thoroughbreds, and often wandered her paddocks and stables. *The New York Times* described her as being "quiet, sardonic, and always patrician."

She had an amicable relationship with the English royal family and would attend the races at Ascot as the guest of Queen Elizabeth II and the Queen Mother.

She was a member of the Aiken Garden Club and chairwoman of various garden clubs, including the National Roadside Council and the roadside committees of the Garden Clubs of America and the Federated Garden Clubs of New York. She had hands-on responsibility for the formal gardens at her Aiken home, Hopelands, which continue to thrive to this very day.

Having seen the development of horse racing in America, by 1962, Mrs. Iselin became disillusioned with the sport in her home country. As quoted in *The New York Times*, she said, "In England racing is conducted by gentlemen. There I am treated like a lady instead of a business corporation." It was around that time that she began to spend May to July in England, then to return to Saratoga.

She continued to spend her winters at Hopelands in Aiken and died there on April 5, 1970 at the age of 102. Her estate was bequeathed to the City of Aiken to be used as a public park. The Aiken Thoroughbred Racing Hall of Fame and Museum today occupies Mrs. Iselin's stables, and holds a treasure trove of mementos, trophies, and history of Aiken-trained thoroughbreds who have gone on to fame on various tracks around the country.

Hope Iselin Jones was born in 1907 and was Hope and C. Oliver Iselin's only surviving child. She gained her mother's love for dogs and horses at the family estates in New York and Aiken. In the 1930s she left for Arizona, where she met a cowboy named Honeycutt Jones, who she married. She bought property in Redfield Canyon located in the Galiuro Mountains, where she and her husband lived. Their property was known as the C-Spear Ranch. They raised horses, but the property quickly became a refuge for wild horses, which they ran on Federal Bureau of Land Management property, ultimately bringing them into conflict with that agency.

Although the marriage ended in divorce, Hope and Honeycutt had one child, a son they named Archer. Hope remained at the C-Spear Ranch for at least ten years, raising her son, but began to spend more time at a small horse ranch she bought near Tucson. She eventually began living in an apartment in Tucson, and only occasionally visited her horse ranch.

Upon gaining adulthood, Archer Iselin Jones married and moved to his grandmother's home state, Rhode Island. He returned to Arizona in 1988 and died of a heart attack while hiking in the Santa Rita Mountains.

Nathanael Greene Herreshoff was born in Bristol, Rhode Island, in 1848, where he began his seventy-two-year career in nautical design. Known for his high standards, he was the most innovative nautical designer of his time, earning him the sobriquet *Wizard of Bristol.*

Revered by the New York Yacht Club as their designer of choice for America's Cup defense, his engineering innovations and designs included *Vigilant*, 1893, on which he was helmsman; *Defender*, 1895; *Columbia*, 1899 and 1901; *Reliance*, 1903; and *Resolute*, 1920. In each case the Herreshoff-designed yacht never failed to win. C. Oliver Iselin was the NYYC's point man and syndicate partner who managed and coordinated with Herreshoff in all Cup designs before 1920. It was through this association that they shared a strong friendship until Iselin's death on New Year's day 1932.

By the 1930s, Herreshoff was spending winters in Coconut Grove, Florida, and was there on the night that his Bristol estate burned to the ground in December 1931, one month before the death of his friend Oliver Iselin.

On June 2, 1938, Herreshoff died in his bed, and as if nature now knew that a nautical genius was gone, it completed the eradication by destroying the Herreshoff Manufacturing Company in the great hurricane of October 1938.

THE HIGHLAND PARK HOTEL

In 1866, a group of investors led by Benjamin Pulaski Chatfield[87] began construction of the Highland Park Hotel. Chatfield, who was president of the Plymouth Granite Company of Waterbury, Connecticut, was aware of Aiken's antebellum reputation as a health resort. Experienced as a stonemason, he built a successful prewar business with his brother, John Lyman Chatfield, better known as Colonel John Lyman Chatfield, of the 6th Connecticut Volunteers. Colonel Chatfield was mortally wounded at the Second Battle of Fort Wagner at Morris Island during the War Between the States in July 1863, and died of his combat wounds in Connecticut on August 9, 1863. He never saw the construction of the Highland Park.

Now that peace had arrived, Benjamin saw a business opportunity in building upon the city's antebellum reputation as a health resort, and directed his marketing efforts to the North, instead of to the war-ruined planters of South Carolina's lowcountry,[88] the group that initially discovered Aiken's curative environment. Some would have considered Benjamin's business enterprise exploitive. Nonetheless, it must have taken courage to make an investment reported to be over $500,000 to build the 250-guest capacity hotel during a time when Aiken was occupied by Union troops, and would continue to be so for ten unpleasant years, during the period known as Reconstruction.

In October 1870, Chatfield recruited Joseph Colton, a British-born naturalized American citizen from Waterbury, Connecticut, to take up the position of steward for his new hotel. Chatfield had known Colton since the war years when he had served with Colonel Chatfield as a medic with the 6th Connecticut Volunteers. Following the war,

---

87   Chatfield would ultimately become the sole proprietor of the Highland Park.
88   Aiken's reputation as a health resort was created by well-heeled SC lowcountry planters who annually escaped the summer heat and the accompanying health perils, such as malaria, by going to Aiken.

Colton had spent time in Washington in the Quartermaster's Office, and the four years before coming to Aiken served as steward at the State Hospital in New Haven, Connecticut.

While Chatfield believed that Aiken's mild fall and winter climate would appeal to northerners seeking to escape harsh winters, and experience the healthful environment that was being publicized in northern newspapers, he also knew that with the railroad now providing service on northern and southern routes, the trip to Aiken would be less onerous. As such, the Highland Park would open in mid-November each year and close in June. It would cater to the well-to-do and offer every convenience possible, and it was routinely booked to capacity during the season. In an attempt to develop summer business using reduced rates as a lure for visitors from Columbia, Charleston, and the lowcountry, Chatfield considered opening the hotel year round on an experimental basis in 1873. During that same year he entered into an agreement to operate the Planters' Hotel in Augusta, and began the task of renovating and reopening the shuttered building. It was evident that his business fortunes were ascending.

Rising four stories, the Highland Park was large, luxurious, and sprawled over twenty-three acres between Highland Park Drive and Hayne Avenue. Its long halls, covered by Brussels carpets, were its arteries servicing the spacious, well-appointed rooms featuring marble-top walnut furniture. Its outside borders of sweeping verandas embraced strolling promenaders every evening, and it boasted a bowling alley and men's and ladies' billiard rooms. The dining room and parlors not only served well-heeled tourists, but also accommodated activities attended by local residents such as local business meetings, fund-raisers, weddings, and community social events. Additionally, winter visitors who owned or leased cottages for the season would often host teas and luncheons at the Highland Park.

The hotel became known for its evening entertainment where occasionally the dining room waiters would put on shows for guests. In fact, the attraction became so popular that it spread to waiters at the Aiken Hotel, and on at least one occasion, waiters from both hotels joined together in a theatrical presentation at the Aiken Town Hall, as reported in the *Aiken Journal* of March 28, 1874. In addition to musicals, the Highland Park was the venue for plays. One noted playwright, Captain Oscar Cole, who was a perennial guest at the Highland Park, had his original play, *Carpetbagger*, performed by local amateurs in the hotel's sixty- by thirty-foot saloon parlor.

Guest conveniences included a Shaving Saloon offering haircuts, shaves, and shampoos. And through Mr. J. Wilkes North, Hotel Railroad Agent, guests could even purchase train tickets to Boston, New York, Savannah, Charleston, and Florida without leaving the hotel lobby. Outdoor sports were offered, including croquet, badminton, hiking, and equestrian activities. While the emphasis was on hygienic cleanliness and promoting a healthful environment, outdoor sporting activities were an important component of the Highland Park experience.

In April 1874, as construction plans were being implemented for the new wing of the hotel, Joseph Colton, who had served as hotel steward for nearly five years, passed away. Abandoning his native city of Waterbury, Connecticut, he adopted Aiken as his hometown and became a cherished member of the Aiken community. His passing was mourned by many friends and business associates not only in Aiken, but also in Augusta, where he served as steward of the Planters' Hotel.[89]

Mr. E. H. Tomlinson replaced Colton as hotel steward and oversaw, along with Chatfield, the construction progress on Highland Park's new addition. It was intended that the new wing would be ready for the 1875 season. The new construction reflected a French architectural style with dormers on the upper floor. Its twenty-five new rooms were contained in a wing that swept in a westward direction, giving an "L" shape to the building. In addition to new accommodations, the construction included renovations to the dining room and kitchen. One contemporary newspaper review glowingly stated, "The plans for heating and lighting are perfect, and the cuisine or cooking department which possesses all the modern improvements is perfection in itself." The new wing did indeed open on schedule in November 1875.

---

89   By this time both hotels were controlled by Benjamin Chatfield.

The year 1876 marked the country's centennial year, and celebrations were seen everywhere around the U.S., and Aiken was no exception. In April Aiken's centennial celebration centered on the Highland Park Hotel grounds, where a commemorative Centennial Tree was planted. The Centennial Tree idea sprung from the state of Michigan and spread throughout the country where many such trees were planted for the occasion. In Aiken there was a Committee of Arrangements and a Ladies Committee that prepared and coordinated a range of activities from singing, readings, speeches by dignitaries, and even a poem was read by Highland Park's perennial visitor playwright, Capt. Oscar Cole, who was designated Governor of the Day. The tree, a *Gigantea sequoia*, was planted by the children who bore it to its location on the grounds. The festive day was followed by a collation with wine in the hotel's saloon parlor.

In the summer of 1876, the hotel underwent further expansion when Mr. Chatfield announced a plan to build several cottages on the Highland Park's grounds. The cottages were to be ready for the 1877 season.

Throughout the 1880s, the Highland Park continued to prosper. During the season it was very seldom that it was not booked to capacity by mostly aristocratic visitors from primarily New York, Massachusetts, Pennsylvania, Connecticut, and Canada.

By the early and mid-1890s, the Highland Park had expanded its management and supervisory personnel. Mr. H. W. Priest had taken over as hotel front manager. A Mr. Eger[90] was responsible for the overall "backroom" of the house, presumably an operational responsibility, and there were numerous supervisors for the various sub-departments.

By this time the Highland Park's stables accommodated fifty horses and had ninety-five lease horses available each season, as driving and riding were the chief amusements of the hotel's guests. Mr. McBee Williams was in charge of the Highland Park's livery stables.

In 1898, Mr. Thomas Fallon was the chief engineer of the Highland Park Hotel.

---

90   Sources differ on the spelling of the operation manager's name: Eger and Eager.

John McGowan hated working the night shift in the hotel's laundry room. He preferred his other responsibility at the Highland Park—night watchman. His real ambition had been to become a deputy sheriff of Aiken County, but he had already been turned down for that job. The official reason was because of his height. At five foot two, and weighing less than 150 pounds, the county sheriff had the perfect reason for keeping him off the force. The real reason was his reputation as a hothead, which stemmed from what some would call "little man syndrome."

John McGowan's family was not without influence in Aiken County, and bending to that pressure, Mr. Eger agreed to hire him at the Highland Park. Eger was in need of a night watchman for fire and security, and also had a need for someone to work in the hotel's laundry. Eger knew of McGowan's personal shortcomings and thought that he could do little harm on the midnight-to-eight shift, where he would have minimal contact with hotel guests. Besides, it was almost impossible to find anyone willing to work the midnight shift for security and fire watch. McGowan was placed in the supervisory care of Thomas Fallon, chief engineer for the hotel. Mr. Eger didn't quite know how to categorize McGowan's dual responsibilities, and because Fallon was responsible for the hotel's plant facilities, including the laundry, it made sense that he should be McGowan's supervisor.

Thomas Fallon was a man who took his responsibilities seriously. He had experience in the various trades associated with the building industry, and had spent many years as a contractor, erecting buildings for private and public agencies. His experience prepared him well for his work at the hotel. When it came to repairs or construction, he excelled. Where he did not excel was in dealing with people; things yes, people no. He was a perfectionist with an authoritarian personality, and it took little time for enmity to surface and fester between himself and McGowan.

One of Fallon's first disagreements with McGowan was over his insistence on wearing a sidearm while making his night watchman rounds. After much harangue, Fallon allowed McGowan to carry a firearm, against his better judgment, but not before giving him a stern warning about his responsibility. McGowan would have carried his Colt .36 caliber Navy revolver anyway, with or without Fallon's approval, because in his mind a firearm was an essential piece of equipment for a night watchman. And because the weapon had been passed on to him by his uncle, a cavalry officer who rode with Hampton's Legion at the second Battle of Bull Run in '62, he wore it with pride and reverence.

The animosity between supervisor and employee continued, but somehow things went along in an acceptable fashion. McGowan was dependable and prompt in reporting to work, not because of his job in the laundry, as he would never have taken the job in the laundry without also being allowed to be night watchman, where he tried to spend most of his shift time. After all, he had Adele, a middle-aged Negro and mother of six, who also worked the night shift in the laundry. She had worked in the laundry for five years and would handle the routine there for the most part, and he would take time from his grounds and hallway patrol to look in on her from time to time and help out when needed. After all, the bulk of the work was done by the laundry's day shift once the housekeepers deposited the previous night's bed linens and towels with them. The night shift only had to deal with tablecloths and napkins from the last dining room closing, and any emergencies that might arise in the late night hours.

Sunday, February 6, 1898

John McGowan reported to work at midnight as usual. It wasn't a pleasant evening as there was a growing chill in the air, and frost was already beginning to form on the Highland Park's lawn. It was early Sunday morning and there were 168 guests registered at the Highland Park. Most guests had turned in early that Saturday, as the evening's chilly weather kept the verandas clear and the rockers empty. By midnight a few were in their rooms enjoying the fireplace warmth with a final brandy, and many others were already asleep.

McGowan started his shift with his usual walk through the dining room, parlor saloon, then down the hotel's long residential halls. He enjoyed patrolling the halls late at night, ensuring that doors were closed and no late night revelry was taking place. He would walk as quietly as possible in hopes of overhearing what muffled intimate sounds, or conversations meant for the very few, that may seep through the fine oak doors.

The chilly nighttime breeze made him want to stay inside, but true to his duty, he walked the verandas and checked the hotel's adjacent stables and cottages. He was glad he brought his leather gloves this evening which gave his hands some relief as he crunched through the frost going from cottage to cottage on his rounds.

In the vast laundry room, clothes washers were operated by a steam engine that turned pulleys that drove belts to turn a wooden drum. Although steam engines are relatively quiet, the laundry was placed in the basement, directly below the hotel's kitchen at the "L" where the new addition met the original building. Since the hotel was heated by steam, that same system drove the "new" clothes washers.[91]

Adele fed the large wood-burning stove that provided the heat necessary to operate the dryers. Ignoring the arthritis in her hands, she pulled the linens from the washers and carefully set them on the drying frames, making sure they were positioned correctly. She had learned to operate the new dryers fairly recently when the hotel added them to its facility. To be dried, clothing or linens would be suspended over frames which would need to be placed in a specific place, at a specific distance from the oven. The frames had to be positioned correctly—too far, and the clothing would not dry; too close, and the risk of fire would ensue. Many of the laundry employees were still learning how to properly operate this new invention,[92] which could only be found in the homes

---

91   In 1858, Hamilton Smith improved upon an original clothes washer design by James King. In 1874, William Blackstone further improved the design, and now machines were steam driven instead of hand cranked.

92   George T. Sampson of Palmyra, NY invented the first clothes dryer in 1892, a ventilator dryer. Clothing would be suspended from a frame in close relation to a heated stove.

of the wealthy or in fine hotels like the Highland Park.

It was 5:15 a.m. and she was now approaching the final couple hours of her shift when the night desk clerk, Mr. W. H. Brooks, came through the laundry room door.

"Adele, would you please take fresh bath linens to room fourteen right away? They just called down and requested them."

"Yassah, Mr. Brooks, but we needs to find Mister John to tend the dryers; dey can't be let alone," exclaimed Adele. "Dey needs to be turned, or we done gonna have fire," she warned.

"Okay, you go on with the linens now, and I'll find McGowan. We can't keep the guests waiting," returned Brooks as he went out the door headed for the main lobby.

Upon arriving in the lobby, he quickly forgot about McGowan.

It was at least fifteen minutes before anyone returned to the laundry.

Mrs. Choate, head laundress, enjoyed coming to work in the early morning hours, and was always first to arrive ahead of the day shift. Following her usual routine, she would first check in with the front desk clerk, then proceed on to her desk, located in the laundry.

It was still dark at 5:30 a.m. in February, but the dying moon still was aglow, lighting up the hotel's white frosted lawn.

McGowan, who was returning from a final check of the cottages, saw something that made him stop dead in his tracks. Looking straight ahead at the "L" junction, he could clearly see plumes of smoke coming from either the laundry or the adjacent waiters' changing room. His heart began to race and his stomach nerves began to tighten as he began a running dash through the frost-encrusted grounds, slipping and falling twice, on his way to the hotel laundry.

At that very same moment, Mrs. Choate was opening the laundry room door and was met by a wall of smoke which billowed out, stinging her eyes and making her cough from the burning sensation in her lungs. Unable to shout, or see, she stumbled back into the hallway in a fit of raucous coughing while continuing to ingest the acrid smoke. She fell to the floor, unable to speak or shout a warning. It all happened in an instant.

The now open laundry room door provided the ventilation for the fire to gain strength, and it began to spread up to the ceiling on its way to the hotel's kitchen, directly above.

Breathless, McGowan arrived at the laundry to find Mrs. Choate on the hallway floor engulfed in a continuous wave of black smoke. His eyes were stinging and his vision failing, and although he was still breathless from the run, he tried, without success, to hold his breath against the certain inhalation of the ubiquitous, stinking smoke. Despite his violent coughing, he helped Mrs. Choate to her feet, and they both stumbled out the exterior door, falling on the ground, choking from the ingested smoke.[93] Their violent coughing continued as they gulped the fresh morning air, but neither of them could yet call for help, and no one else was yet aware of the fire which was now spreading to the adjacent waiters' dressing room and the kitchen above.

Head Chef Alexis Bordel, who had just arrived to the kitchen, was making initial preparations for the morning breakfast. The hotel's chief baker, Charles Klein, was also there. Bordel, who had come from England two years prior, was proud of his modern American kitchen. It was far more advanced than the one at Wentworth House in New Castle, his previous employer.

As Bordel approached the large commercial icebox in the far corner of the kitchen, the area that sat directly above the laundry, he thought he could smell smoke. He glanced out the window overlooking the southwest lawn and saw black smoke rising from below, now directly outside his kitchen window. He thought he could hear the crackle of flame eating wood coming from below his feet.

"Fire, fire!" he shouted at the top of his lungs as he grabbed Klein by the shoulder and made a dash to the door, then a long, winded sprint through the dining room, parlor saloon, and the lobby, arriving at the front desk. "Fire, fire, Mr. Brooks, call…volunteers quick!" he sputtered while he and Klein were trying to catch their breath. In broken sentences Bordel continued, "Fire…from the…the laundry…

---

93   One newspaper reported that Mrs. Choate escaped by jumping through the first-floor window, which would have been ground level since the laundry was located in the basement.

call volunteers!"

Mr. Brooks immediately went to the fire warning bell located just outside the lobby entrance, and began to furiously pump the handle, starting a clang! clang! clang! which everyone knew could only mean one thing—fire! The bell could be heard in town, and members of Aiken's Fire Company #1 were awakened by the clanging coming from the direction of the Highland Park Hotel.

Brooks recruited Chef Bordel to remain and continue working the bell as he dashed, with Klein in tow, down the residential hall to awaken sleeping guests.

"Mr. Klein, take the lower corridor, and I'll begin with the upper floors. Knock on every door until you have a response, and order them to evacuate immediately," instructed Brooks.

As day shift personnel were beginning to report for work, Chef Bordel hurriedly directed each to knock on doors and help guests remove personal valuables, don warm clothing, and evacuate immediately. Only after all guests were evacuated would they, circumstances permitting, remove valuable hotel furniture. Responding to the fire bell, which was now being sounded by a member of the housekeeping staff, local citizens began arriving on the scene. Bordel, ill trained for such work, but singularly pressed into duty by circumstances, became the de facto emergency manager, directing employees and local citizen-volunteers who were now coming to the aid of the Highland Park.

Fortunately, the fire began at the "L" confluence of the hotel's two wings. It was a slow-spreading fire, taking some time to arrive to populated areas of the hotel. The fire's delay allowed guests to evacuate the building, some wrapped in blankets, some carrying suitcases, some carrying golf clubs, tennis racquets, and other favorite and valuable *equipage.*

Hotel employees helped guests down the stairs and corridors and out onto the frosty lawn, while the now climbing, rolling banks of smoke coming from the Highland Park could be seen from the furthest reaches of town. Aiken's Hook and Ladder Company #1 was on the scene and manning the water stands, which were low on water.

John McGowan, having recovered from smoke inhalation, was working with firemen and manning one of the four hoses now trained upon the hotel's "L." It was cold and the water froze McGowan's and the other hose-wielding firemen's hands.

The fast-thinking breakfast waiters who had arrived for work had the presence of mind to run into the hotel's liquor storeroom and rescue some of the finer liquors, bourbons, and champagnes and were cheerfully dispensing the warming beverages among the guests who were now milling about the hotel lawn, watching the Highland Park go up in flames. The assembled audience was made up of many northern aristocrats, including Clarence Dolan and family of Newport and Philadelphia; Mr. J. Foxhall Keene, close friend to William Vanderbilt, Jr.; Mr. E. H. English, of New Haven, a touring golf professional; William E. Iselin and family, of New York; Mr. J. Lewis Stackpole of Boston; Dr. William Appleton of Harvard Medical School, Boston; Mr. J. B. Tilton and family of Cincinnati; Mr. Gary Phelps Dodge; and Mr. M. A. Meyer of Chicago, among others. There were 168 guests at the hotel, all of whom became homeless on this fateful day.

"Here, John, take this to warm yourself," said one of the waiters as he handed McGowan a full glass of bourbon.

"Francis, you know that I don't partake of alcohol, but this water and frost—I am freezing!" he returned.

"Come on, John, come sit over here, it will warm you," insisted the waiter.

With reluctance, McGowan gave up his hose to a nearby volunteer and followed the waiter to a quiet, far corner of the property where he sat and drank down the entire glass. It took only minutes before a warm glow stirred in his body and a light-headed swirl began to envelop his brain; effects that would be expected to a body unused to alcohol consumption.

As McGowan sat, somewhat enjoying his alcohol-induced spin, a hard-charging Thomas Fallon, McGowan's supervisor, was fast approaching with a clear display of anger on his face.

"Where were you, McGowan?" demanded an angry, red-faced

Fallon. "Why were you not in the laundry, where you were supposed to be, when the fire broke out? You could have done something to stop it, or at least have given everyone an early warning. We're going to lose the entire building because of you!" Fallon continued with his finger pointing, in an angry, menacing manner.

What happened next was witnessed by few, as the crowd's collective face, with backs turned to the two quarreling employees, was focused on the burning building,.

McGowan, in one motion, leaped to his feet and said, while reaching for the Navy revolver on his hip, "I've had enough of you." And in the blink of an eye, he drew, cocked, and fired in the direction of Thomas Fallon's chest. Reacting quickly, Fallon managed to turn slightly but was still hit. He staggered backward a few steps and fell in a heap of anguish. The loud report of the .36 caliber drew the attention of everyone milling about before the hotel, and now all eyes turned and fixed on the figure of John McGowan, with revolver still in hand, hunched over a writhing Thomas Fallon in the far corner of the Highland Park Hotel's expansive lawn.

THE REST OF THE STORY

McGowan and Fallon in fact were the subject of an ancillary article[94] about the fire, printed in the *Augusta Chronicle* newspaper of February 7th 1898 as follows:

> *After the fire, Chief Engineer, Thomas Fallon and John McGowan, a young fellow employed in the laundry got into a dispute, presumably over responsibility for the origin of the fire and McGowan shot Fallon in the breast. Fortunately for Fallon it was only a flesh wound, the bullet plowing across from one side of his chest to the*

---

94   *The New York Times* also reported the following in its February 7th article "Hotel Burned at Aiken, S.C.": *In the excitement of the fire Thomas Fallon of Boston was shot and badly wounded by one of the hotel engineers.* The incorrect implication of this story is that Fallon was a guest at the hotel.

other under the skin outside of the breast bone, and doing no harm.

It is said McGowan got wet fighting the fire, and was given too much whiskey to warm him up. All parties were very reticent and tried to hush the matter up declaring it was only an accidental shooting.

The Highland Park Hotel was reduced to smoldering wreckage by noon of that same day, the speed of its destruction aided by high winds. All that remained were the fireplace chimneys. At some point during the fire a telegraph message was sent to the Augusta Fire Company requesting aid, and later a dispute surfaced that the request was not sent in time for any assistance to make a difference, although a fire company from Augusta did arrive on the scene. The fire was confined to the main building. The stables and cottages were untouched, except for some paint blistering on the sides closest to the hotel. No guests were injured by the fire, and most of their personal belongings were saved, thanks to the fire's slow growth in its early stage. An *Augusta Chronicle* newspaper reporter on the scene noted that "handsome furniture, pianos, iron bedsteads, featherbeds, and numerous other articles of hotel furnishings and luxuries lay strewn about. Here and there a tennis racquet, and yonder a caddy of golf sticks told of the sports that had a top place to them so far as those were concerned who had been guests of the house."

Benjamin P. Chatfield's ownership role at the time of the fire appears to have been diminished. At the time of the fire, a Mr. J. H. Whittimore of Naugatuck, Connecticut, owned half of the bonds and stock of the Highland Park Hotel Company. A Mr. Franklin Farrell of Ansonia, Connecticut, and H. H. Peck of Waterbury, who also served as president of the company, each owned a quarter. These individuals became involved with the expansion of the original hotel, which was controlled by Chatfield at that time. In those early years of the expansion, the Highland Park defaulted on its interest payments and was almost forced into foreclosure, except for a satisfactory agreement that was reached among the parties, which saved it. Whittimore estimated the loss at $155,000 with only $98,000 covered by insurance. In March 1899, one year following the fire, Chatfield was appointed postmaster of Aiken and served in that capacity until his death on April 3, 1901.

Guests of the Highland Park Hotel who were displaced by the fire found quarters in various places. With every hotel room in the city otherwise filled, a number of them moved into the Bon Air Hotel in Augusta, some were taken in by Aiken friends, and others became guests of hospitable Aikenites who they met for the first time. It was reported that Mr. William C. Whitney, of Joye Cottage, provided lodging within his twenty-four guest rooms for certain fire refugees. The list of displaced persons included some prominent names from major northern cities who were perennial visitors to the Highland Park, a beloved hotel they were to never see again.

THE SPEAKER'S FINAL VISIT TO AIKEN

"You know, Charles, no longer being Speaker of the House eventually would have killed him anyway. He lived, breathed, and absolutely loved it," said Alice Roosevelt Longworth to her husband's manservant, Charles Eichoff.

She made the statement while leaving the Spring Grove Cemetery in Cincinnati, Ohio, knowing that Republicans had recently received a dousing in the midterm elections due to economic conditions in the country. As such they would no longer be the dominant party in the House of Representatives and would consequently lose the Speakership.

Mrs. Longworth was at Spring Grove on Saturday, April 11, 1931 to bury her husband, Nicholas Longworth, who had died on April 9th at the Hayne Avenue, Aiken home of James and Laura Curtis. Many had come to the cemetery that day to pay their last respects, including President Hoover and numerous Republican representatives and senators from around the country, and a few Democrats. Even George White, the Democratic governor of Ohio, was present, but conspicuously absent was another Democrat, the governor of New York, Alice's cousin, Franklin D. Roosevelt. He had sent his condolences but begged off due to urgent state business which required him to be in Albany.

As she stepped into the limousine, Alice began to think about Nicholas's life, political career, and their very untraditional marital relationship. She kept a few confidants throughout the years, including Senator William Borah[95] of Idaho and Charles Eichoff, Nicholas's servant for thirty-one years. Her relationship with Borah was more than platonic, versus Eichoff, who made a good, sympathetic sounding board for whatever was on her mind. She didn't much care for

---

95   A staunch supporter of Prohibition, Republican William Borah served in the U.S. Senate 1907–1940. He was an intimate friend and confidant to Alice Roosevelt Longworth.

Nicholas's drinking cronies in the House of Representatives, as she detested his drinking and was an advocate of Prohibition. However, she was neutral about his female companions. Although unspoken, they mutually acquiesced to an open marriage.

Unlike many lifelong Republicans, Nicholas Longworth was everyone's friend. He was one of those rare politicians who, because of his gregarious, jovial, and optimistic personality garnered support on certain issues from both sides of the political spectrum. He was a charmer and had a way to make people like him. One of his best friends and drinking buddies was Texas Democrat "Cactus Jack" Garner,[96] House minority leader. There were many times the two would pass the evening at the "Bureau of Education,"[97] located in the basement of the Capitol Building.

Charles Eichoff accompanied Alice on the ride back to Rookwood, the family's hundred-acre Cincinnati estate.

"Charles, I never really minded him traveling to Aiken these past three years," said Alice to an attentive Eichoff. "He liked to ride but wasn't really a horseman, or a polo player, but he did like women, liquor, poker, and his violin. Meeting his death in Aiken with friends and particularly the women he loved seems fitting," she continued with detachment. "Nick was a great father to Paulina and never questioned me about Bill.[98] Paulina was the only thing he loved more than being Speaker of the House."

Alice had a demeanor and way of expressing herself that could at times reflect a suspicious, distrustful, but what others would call a "stoic" personality. She was witty and had mastered the sarcastic retort, and had been accused by societal matrons, columnists, and other observers

---

96   John "Cactus Jack" Garner served in Congress 1903–1933. He became Speaker of the House following Longworth's death, and remained as such until he was elected the 32nd vice president of the U.S. in 1933, running with Franklin Delano Roosevelt, and served with Roosevelt until 1941.

97   Unknown to the outside world, the "Bureau of Education" was a sanctuary located under the Capitol Building in the 1920s, where many congressmen and senators would gather to imbibe in imported, bootlegged liquor, despite Prohibition being the law of the land.

98   Senator William "Bill" Borah fathered Alice's daughter Paulina (pronounced with a long i), who was born in 1925. Nicholas was suspicious of Paulina's paternity, but nonetheless lovingly accepted her.

of holding a cynical view of the people she encountered in politics and society. The oft-repeated statement that was credited to her, *If you have nothing good to say, come sit by me,* was indicative of the image she created for herself. There were some who believed that her defensive personality, which seemed to be rooted in self-preservation, stemmed from the first three years of her life. Both her mother and grandmother died within two days of her birth, and for the next three years, her father Theodore Roosevelt, would have nothing to do with her. She was raised during that time by Roosevelt's sister, known as "Auntie Bye," who was to be the only person to give her unconditional love throughout her life. Roosevelt never spoke to daughter Alice about her mother, and what she learned later in life came from Auntie Bye.

Nicholas Longworth III was born in Cincinnati, Ohio, on November 5th 1869 and was the eldest child of Nicholas Longworth II and Susan Walker Longworth. Nicholas Longworth II came from a wealthy and prominent Cincinnati family. He was a lawyer and served for a time on the Ohio Supreme Court. His wife, Susan Walker, was the daughter of Judge Timothy Walker, the founding dean of the Cincinnati Law School.

Young Nicholas had had all the advantages a young man could ask for in his youth. He was musically inclined and earnestly began studying the violin at an early age. As a child, he was not allowed to play contact sports to ensure that his valuable violinist's hands would not be injured. In later years he was considered by touring professional violinists, including Efrem Zimbalist, to be the finest amateur in the country.

In keeping with family tradition, he attended Harvard College, but wanted to come home for law school where he obtained his degree from Cincinnati Law School in 1894. Immediately after graduation he was admitted to the Ohio bar, began a law practice, and by 1898 found himself on the City's Board of Education.

His political career had begun!

As the limousine wended its way through the narrow cemetery

lanes out onto the highway for the trip back to Rookwood, Alice continued her soliloquy to a silent Charles Eichoff.

"I remember when Nick came to Washington in '03 for his first term in Congress. I was nineteen years old and he was thirty-three, but that didn't matter as I've always preferred older men. He was the most eligible bachelor in Washington, and at that time, I thought I'd never find the right man. Well, from the three-year perspective before our wedding, he certainly seemed like the right man, and for the first six years[99] of our marriage, it went well. But blood is thicker than water, and I could never forgive him for siding with William Howard Taft against Father in 1912.[100] Things personally changed for us then, and I rejoiced in the fact that he lost his seat in Congress that year,"[101] she said.

Aiken, South Carolina
Ten days earlier

Despite the fact that he was suffering from a severe and persistent cold that he had contracted in the final days of the congressional session, Nicholas was determined to escape the rigors of Washington and left for Aiken as planned, on March 30[th.]

Waiting for him at the Aiken Station were two close friends, Laura Curtis,[102] who had extended the invitation to him for a visit to her

---

99   Alice, who was Theodore Roosevelt's daughter, married Longworth in a1906 White House ceremony.

100   Taft received the Republican Party nomination, and T. Roosevelt, a Republican, ran as an independent in his so-called Progressive "Bull Moose" Party. Nick supported Taft the conservative Republican over his father-in-law, for which Alice never forgave him.

101   Longworth lost his Congressional seat by 105 votes in 1912. Alice took pleasure in publicizing that she was responsible for at least 100 of those votes. This was in retaliation for his support of her father's presidential opponent. Nicholas regained his seat in 1914.

102   Laura Merriam Curtis was the daughter of William Merriam, who had been governor of Minnesota and later director of the census. In 1912, she married James Curtis, the assistant secretary of the U.S. Treasury. They were divorced in 1924, remarried one another in 1925, and were divorced a second time in 1938.

Hayne Avenue home, and Alice Olin Dows,[103] Longworth's poetry-writing mistress. Laura and Alice maintained homes in New York and Washington, and it was through the Washington society circle that Nicholas met these women.

"There he is, there he is!" said Alice with excitement to Laura as they spotted their friend disembarking with the other passengers from the Southern Railway passenger car.

"Nick, oh Nick, we're over here!" called Laura from the top of the platform.

With handkerchief in hand, a coughing Longworth descended the steps of the railroad car and broke out into a big grin upon seeing his two friends, who were now waving to attract his attention. None of the other passengers or any of the platform workers paid any special attention to him. That was what he liked about Aiken—anonymity!

As he approached, his friends excitedly trotted on over to greet him.

"Laura, Alice, what a pleasure to see you. No welcome kisses today, I'm afraid, as I'm battling a very bad cold, and I'm sure it is quite contagious," he said as he greeted the ladies with a hoarse voice that had progressively gotten worse over the past week.

"We have lots of things planned this coming week to make you feel better, Nick! Did you bring your violin?" asked Alice with enthusiasm. "We've planned a dinner tomorrow evening in your honor, and we were hoping that you would favor us with some of your beautiful music," she added.

"I never travel anywhere without my violin, Alice, and yes, I would feel privileged to entertain with a few melodies, perhaps after dinner," he returned.

On the second evening of Nicholas's visit, the Curtises hosted a dinner with a very limited Aiken winter colonist guest list, all of whom had societal roots in Washington and New York. Evalyn Walsh

---

103 Alice Olin Dows was the daughter of the famous New York attorney Stephen H. Olin. She was married to the wealthy importer/exporter/real estate businessman Tracy Dows from 1903 until his death in 1937.

McLean[104] was present. Nick had visited her Washington home, Friendship, for the first time while on his honeymoon, when she and Ned were also newlyweds. He liked Evalyn and they remained good friends for many years, even after her split with Ned. Accompanying Evalyn was Joseph Alsop[105] from Georgetown, the historic district of Washington. Although Alsop was a syndicated columnist for the *New York Herald Tribune*, he was a Longworth ally and a strong Republican. Alsop always stayed at the Willcox whenever visiting Aiken.

Winthrop and Lucy Rutherfurd of Berrie Road also were guests. When she was still Lucy Mercer, she had been a dinner guest at the Longworth home in Washington. Originally from Baltimore, Lucy had been living in Washington since before the '20s. She and Alice Roosevelt had been friends before her marriage to Nicholas, and the friendship continued many years after. Nick's two friends, Dwight F. Davis,[106] former secretary of war and current governor general of the Philippines, and Daniel J. Duckett, were also present.

With Alice Dows' help, Laura planned every detail of the three-course dinner prepared by the Curtis's domestic staff. She kept the guest list small to afford an intimacy and an informality that sometimes is lost with larger social events.

The dinner conversation was lively and eventually turned to politics, with everyone asking the Speaker if he thought the fallout would continue on the Republican Party since Mr. Hoover was now being blamed for the stock market crash and the ensuing depression, even though many of the economic conditions that set the disaster in motion were not of his doing and out of his control.

"I can assure you of one thing," said Nick to the assembled guests. "Because of the midterm election results, I have finished my last session as Speaker of the House. Our Democrat friends will be taking over, but there is some consolation, and that is Jack Garner, a Texas Democrat

---

104 Evalyn is known for her ownership of the Hope Diamond, and her husband Ned was the heir to the *Washington Post* and *Cincinnati Enquirer* newspapers.

105 Alsop was a distant cousin of Alice Roosevelt Longworth.

106 Davis was an avid tennis player and played at Wimbledon and as a member of the U.S. Team at the turn of the century. The Davis Cup, so named for him, is the trophy given to the winner of an international tennis competition.

and my dear friend, is almost certain to become Speaker. I know I can work with him and some of the other Democrats that I've befriended over the years."

"Which Democrat do you think will receive the presidential nomination at their convention next year?" asked Lucy Mercer Rutherfurd.

"Why, Lucy, I would be very surprised if it's not my wife Alice's cousin and your former employer—Franklin Roosevelt. He's gained a lot of momentum within his party since becoming governor of New York, and I'll be very surprised if there is anyone in the Democratic Party who can command the number of delegates needed to surpass him at the convention. But, he'll get no support from my wife. She's never liked that branch of her family, especially Eleanor, who she's publicly criticized in the past," said Nick.

Throughout the dinner Nick could feel waves of heat beginning to vex his forehead, accompanied by fatigue as he tried to suppress his coughing with limited success. Nonetheless, he would not disappoint his friends and took up his violin to entertain the group, who were now gathered in the Curtis cottage library enjoying postprandial beverages. Nick loved Beethoven and Mendelssohn and played excerpts from both composers' violin concertos, much to the delight of his rapt audience. Little did he know that this would be his last performance!

Despite passing a restless night marked by sweats and chills, he rose at his usual time, fully ignoring the growing symptoms that he interpreted as a chest cold. The Curtis's domestic staff had prepared a sumptuous breakfast, but he had little appetite.

"Nick, I've arranged for you to play golf this morning with George Herbert Walker[107] and Oliver Iselin[108] at the Palmetto Club," said Laura, as she finished her second cup of coffee.

Nick did his best on the golf course that morning and enjoyed the

---

107   George Herbert Walker was an early member of Aiken's Palmetto Golf Club. He was a banker and an investment executive. He was also president of the U.S. Golf Association, and the Walker Cup is named for him. He was also the grandfather of U.S. President George Herbert Walker Bush.

108   C. Oliver Iselin was a wealthy yachtsman from New York. He led the American team to victory on a number of occasions in America's Cup racing. He passed his winters at Hopelands on Whiskey Road.

company of Walker and Iselin as they were in tune with the politics of the day, and chatted optimistically about business conditions during this time of national economic crisis. However, after only four holes Nick needed to quit. He had fatigued due to his growing illness, and the frequency of his coughing had increased and deepened to the point where he was now discharging blood-spotted mucus.

Arriving back at the Curtis's cottage, Nick begged off the afternoon bridge game that Laura had planned, in favor of napping in the guest room. He was sorry to miss it because he knew from past card games with Laura, Alice Dows, and their circle of friends that the focus was more on imbibing fine liquors rather than cards. Even during the "heart years" of prohibition, their little group had gained a Washington reputation for carrying on "wet" parties, and it was no secret that alcohol topped the list of Nick's weaknesses.

Nick's lethargy continued and late Sunday afternoon, April 5th, Laura's level of concern grew to the point that she should take some action. She now strongly suspected that Nick's illness was no ordinary cold, as he insisted it was.

"Nick, should I call Dr. Wilds?" asked Laura with genuine concern.

"No, I'll be fine, I just need some rest, and a bit of time to make this cold go away," he responded in between fits of coughing.

"I can go to the druggist for some Aspironal.[109] Would you like me to do that?" she asked, trying to be helpful.

"That would be good, Laura, thank you," he said, not wanting to disappoint or discourage her helpful concern for his condition.

Nick had taken a tall glass of Irish whiskey before going to his room. What he thought would be a nap turned into an all-night sleep from which he would not awaken until late Monday morning. Upon opening his eyes, he saw Alice Dows sitting by his beside with book in hand.

"Alice, how long have you been here?" he asked groggily.

"Most of the night," she responded.

---

109   Aspironal was a contemporary brand of elixir sold as cough and cold medicine. Some cough/cold remedies of the time contained morphine or cocaine which could be bought over the counter.

She tried to hide her emotional reaction as she surveyed Longworth's gray pallor, sunken eyes, and obvious shortness of breath. She cradled his head with her arm and bent down and kissed his cheek as a tear came to the corner of her eye. She loved Nick more than anyone, and she knew that his situation was far more serious than a "cold," as he described it.

"I love you, dear, but I need to sleep, so tired..." He then fell back into a coma-like sleep.

By Monday afternoon, Laura and Alice were convinced that Nick's condition was extremely serious and so contacted Dr. Wilds, who also lived on Hayne Avenue. Wilds immediately came to the Curtis cottage, listened to the women describe their observations of the past few days, and immediately examined Longworth. Wilds contacted Dr. Thomas Brooks, also of Aiken, and they jointly brought in Dr. V. P. Sydenstricker, a specialist practicing in Augusta. Each doctor examined Longworth. On Monday evening Sydenstricker delivered their opinion to Laura and Alice.

"Ladies, I am sorry to say that we believe that Mr. Longworth is in the advanced stages of lobar pneumonia.[110] His lungs are filled with fluid. The bacteria has attacked his lungs' lobes, multiplied, and advanced to a stage that he will soon be unable to breathe. We will order nurses to assist in monitoring him, and continue to do whatever we can for him, but it is our joint opinion that he may die within the next few days," said Sydenstricker. "You should contact his family immediately," he added.

Both Laura and Alice were dumbstruck with this revelation. They stood in silence, trying to comprehend what they had just heard. They did not want to believe, but knew they must. How could this happen to Nick? — Or to them?

From this point on, Longworth was attended by the three physicians, who would not leave his bedside. They were aided by four nurses

---

110 In lobar pneumonia, bacteria attack the lung's lobe and reproduce, causing an infection. Inflammation of the alveoli (tiny sacs in the lungs that exchange gases) makes them inflexible as the body tries to fight off the bacteria. They fill with fluid and the lungs are unable to take oxygen into the blood and remove carbon dioxide from the blood.

who also attended.

On Tuesday, April 7th, Laura Curtis contacted Alice Roosevelt Longworth and relayed the doctors' opinion of her husband's medical condition. She immediately left Washington for Aiken. Accompanying her was Charles Eichoff, Mildred Reeves, who was Nick's secretary, and a nurse. Alice informed President Hoover of the situation, and he directed his military aide, Colonel Campbell Hodges, to go to Aiken immediately and render whatever assistance was necessary. Before leaving Washington, Alice notified her stepbrothers, Kermit and Archibald Roosevelt, and they made arrangements to immediately leave for Aiken.

News reporters from New York, Washington, and elsewhere quickly learned of the unfolding situation and converged on Aiken. For the next two days, the eyes of the entire country would be focused on this small resort town in South Carolina.

Alice Longworth arrived in Aiken on Wednesday, April 8th and went straight to the Curtis cottage on Hayne Avenue. She attended her husband's bedside and he appeared to rally at midday, but as evening approached, his condition deteriorated.

During the night on Wednesday, his condition worsened, and on Thursday morning April 9th at 10:52 a.m., the beloved Speaker of the House, the People's Speaker, died.

Alice was not at his side when his final moments came. Dr. Wilds, who was present, raised the window shade in Nick's bedroom. This was a prearranged signal to the newsmen that the Speaker of the House was dead. Dr. Wilds made this arrangement in order to minimize strain on the family from the teaming crowd of newsmen outside, clamoring for every detail as the situation progressed.

Colonel Hodges immediately notified President Hoover, who had anticipated this turn of events and had a special train ready to begin making its way to Aiken. Aiken winter colonist millionaire Charles W. Clark[111] ordered his private railroad car "Errant" to be connected to

---

111   Charles Clark was a millionaire businessman who inherited a fortune from his father, who was U.S. Senator William A. Clark of Montana (1901–1907). He was known as the "Copper King," for his wide holdings in mining and the mineral trade.

the government's train upon arrival in Aiken. Since Longworth was not eligible to lie in state, nor was he a veteran, it made no sense to send the train to Washington. His wife ordered that Longworth's body be transported directly to his hometown, Cincinnati.

At 11:00 on Friday morning, the Speaker's body, having been placed aboard a horse-drawn hearse, was taken from the Curtis cottage to Aiken's railroad depot. Mr. D. M. George of Aiken assisted in making the funeral arrangements. Aiken's mayor, W. H. Weatherford, ordered all businesses closed, and the streets were lined with people to watch the somber cortege pass.

Alice Longworth allowed Laura Curtis and Alice Dows to join the funeral party on the train to Cincinnati. Although they arrived by airplane, her Roosevelt stepbrothers did not arrive in time to witness Nicholas' last moment. They also joined the funeral party aboard the train. As the train passed through South Carolina and bordering states, people lined the track with hats in hand, head bowed as they paid last respects to the People's Speaker.

On Saturday morning at seven o'clock, the funeral train arrived in Ohio City, and the body was taken directly to Christ Church for services followed by interment at Spring Grove Cemetery, Cincinnati.

THE REST OF THE STORY

Nicholas Longworth was married to Alice Roosevelt for twenty-five years (1906–1931). When Nicholas arrived in Washington in 1903 as a congressman from the 1st Congressional District of Ohio, he already had a playboy reputation, and was the city's premier *bon vivant.* Alice Roosevelt was well aware of his reputation during their courtship; however, they got on well together. Alice was considered high spirited and "unconventional," and because of this she attracted a good deal of attention from, and popularity with, news reporters. Now Nick entered the spotlight. Longworth was favored by Theodore Roosevelt as son-in-law because they were both Harvard graduates, and more importantly they were both members of the exclusive Harvard club

"Porcellian Society."

The couple enjoyed domestic stability for the first six years of their marriage. However, in 1912, Nicholas supported a Longworth family friend and fellow Ohioan, William Howard Taft, who ultimately gained the Republican nomination for president, over his father-in-law, Theodore Roosevelt, who was snubbed by Republican Party delegates. Being denied the nomination, he tried to regain the presidency by running as a Progressive independent in his so-called "Bull Moose Party." Alice was infuriated by her husband's support choice, and this marked the beginning of the détente which turned into detachment in their marriage.

Longworth was a heavy drinker for most of his life and was attracted to women. He carried on a number of affairs before and after his marriage. He was discreet in his relationships, and it is not known just how much of his private life was known to Alice; however, his philandering was an open secret, and a number of his mistresses were known throughout Washington's societal circle.

The following story has been told about Longworth, which demonstrates his quick wit and his penchant for women. It was circulated in the Capitol, and later became known to the general public:

One day, while lounging in a chair at the Capitol, another member of the House of Representatives ran his hand over Longworth's bald pate and commented, "Nice and smooth. Feels just like my wife's bottom." Longworth felt his own head and returned the answer: "Yes, so it does."

As Speaker of the House (1925–1931), Longworth brought a prestige and authority back to the position that had been eroded over the years by previous Speakers. He had a reputation as a benevolent despot in carrying out his official duties and was able to get things done. His success was partially due to his magnetic and optimistic personality, which he used to his advantage when dealing with members of his own party and those of the opposition.

Although trained as a musician, politics proved to be Longworth's strength as demonstrated by his long thirty-two-year career in both Ohio State and national elected office.

It was his fourth visit to Aiken at the time of his death at age sixty-one.

Alice Roosevelt Longworth enjoyed the national spotlight she found herself under after her father, Theodore Roosevelt, gained the White House through the assassination and death of President William McKinley in 1901. Her father was elected president in his own right in 1904, and she was adopted by the nation as "America's Daughter." Newspapers reported daily (which she encouraged) on her every activity. Her debut into society took place at the White House on January 3, 1902. It was the first debutante ball to take place there, and it catapulted Alice even further into the national spotlight, as she now was invited to take leading parts in national (laying cornerstones, etc.) and international events (she performed the dedication of Germany's Kaiser Wilhelm's new yacht, *Meteor*, which was built in the U.S.).

Although Alice enjoyed her new celebrity status, she wanted to be out on her own, and the only way to do so was through marriage. Besides, debutantes were expected to marry within a couple of years of their coming out, or gossip would begin to spread. Alice had another reason for wanting to be out on her own, and it involved her stepmother Edith. As she admitted in later years, Alice wanted to be free of the ambivalent and sometimes contentious relationship that intermittently existed between herself and her stepmother. She felt that she represented Theodore's first love, her biological mother, and that Edith would like to forget that she was Theodore's second wife.

It was this same feeling, combined with the scars of her abandonment by her father during the first three years of her life, that fostered a maverick, independent personality style that Alice maintained throughout her life.

Alice had comparatively little education beyond her early years, but this was overcome by self-education and an insatiable inquisitiveness in many areas, particularly writing, literature, and languages in later years. She was responsible for launching the career of James Michener, who went on to become a premier historical novelist, and she enjoyed hobnobbing with other writers of note.

Alice never remarried after the death of Nicholas Longworth, but continued to inject herself into politics as an informal power broker (never as a candidate as she had a fear of public speaking), and frequently appeared in other areas of national publicity. News reporters loved her quick wit, iconoclastic opinions of people (usually politicians), current events, places, and many of her utterances were nationally reported with relish.

In 1962, Alice, who had developed an amicable relationship with President John F. Kennedy, was pleased when he signed a bill to name the Longworth House Office Building after Nick. Kennedy admired Alice's father, and she was invited a number of times to the Kennedy White House. At a particular event at the White House in 1962, Alice was present for the unveiling of the restored "bison mantel," an accessory that had been put in place by Theodore Roosevelt.

Alice visited Aiken twice as far as is known; once before her marriage to Nicholas Longworth, and again to claim his body upon his death there. On February 20, 1980, Alice was to meet the same fate as her husband. She died at her home following a brief illness that was determined to be pneumonia; she was ninety-six years of age.

Laura Merriam Curtis was a socialite with ties to Boston, New York, and Washington society. In addition to homes in those cities, the Curtises maintained a winter home on Hayne Avenue in Aiken. Married in 1912, she was the wife of James F. Curtis, a New York attorney who became assistant secretary of the Treasury under President William Howard Taft.

In 1924, Laura Curtis obtained a divorce from Curtis in Paris, France, a city where both had residences.

According to Stacy A. Cordery, professor of history at Monmouth College, as noted in her book *Alice: Alice Roosevelt Longworth, from White House Princess to Washington Power Broker,* he (Nicholas Longworth) was also keeping company throughout the decade (prohibition) with his "girls"—Alice Dows, Laura Curtis, Marie Beale, and Cornelia Mayo.

Cordery also maintains that Longworth's invitation to Aiken came solely from Laura. She was part of a coterie of Longworth consorts and admirers.

Laura's 1924 divorce from James was short-lived as the couple reconciled and were remarried in May 1925. The marriage continued until January 1938 when they divorced a second and final time. Also in that year Laura married John Messick Gross of York, Pennsylvania. Gross was a vice president of the Bethlehem Steel Company.

It is reported that Laura exhibited more grief at Longworth's funeral than wife Alice.

Laura Curtis's daughter, also named Laura, who had attended the Fermata School in Aiken, would marry George H. "Pete" Bostwick in October 1933. Pete Bostwick, a wealthy New Yorker and a highly respected polo player whose family also maintained a home in Aiken, was the grandson of Jabez Bostwick, who was associated with the Rockefellers in the Standard Oil Company.

Alice Dows was the wife of Tracy Dows, a real estate developer in New York who had won renown for developing Fox Hollow estate, and the owner of America's oldest hostelry, The Beekman Arms, at Rhinebeck, New York. Dows was also the heir to his family's import/export business, which had been established for generations.

Alice was a well-known member of New York and Washington society and an ardent supporter of the performing arts. She loved to hear Nicholas Longworth play the violin, and shared a passion for music with him.

The fact that she was a very intimate member of his circle of female friends is evident in a revelation made by her to author Gore Vidal, as reported by Vidal:

When Nicholas Longworth died in 1931, Alice Dows told me how well Alice Longworth had behaved. "She asked me to go with her in the private train that took Nick back to Ohio. Oh, it was very moving. Particularly the way Alice treated me, as if I was the widow, which I suppose I was." She paused; then the handsome, square-jawed face broke into a smile and she used the Edwardian phrase: "Too killing."

It is unknown if Alice Dows ever returned to Aiken following Nicholas Longworth's death there on April 9, 1931.

Aiken Map

1. **Astor Home**
   (extant)
2. **Iselin Home**
   (not extant)
3. **Highland Park Hotel**
   (not extant)
4. **Clinkscale Home**
   (extant)
5. **Beach Home**
   (extant)

(author's map)

The Astor home located at 325 Colleton Avenue is across the street from where the Vanderbilt home once stood. Madeleine Astor's last know visit to Aiken was in 1916. The home later became known as the "Finley Henderson" home.

(author's collection)

RMS Titanic's maiden voyage from Southampton began shortly after noon on April 10, 1912. White Star Lines Director, Bruce Ismay, who was on board, goaded Captain James Smith to try for a new speed record for trans-Atlantic crossing, paying little heed to iceberg warnings. *(public domain)*

Titanic's luxurious dining room provided the setting for a sumptuous dinner hosted by the Wideners and attended by the Astors and other members of society, a short time before the ship's fatal encounter with the berg. *(public domain)*

During his first marriage to Ava Lowle Willing, John Jacob Astor IV became an Aiken winter colonist occupying what would become known as the "Finley Henderson" home located at 325 Colleton Avenue.

He was 47 years of age at the time of his second marriage to 18 year old Madeleine Force in September 1911, an event that shocked New York society. Following the very private nuptials in Newport, Rhode Island, the newlyweds left for Europe to evade the firestorm of societal criticism and gossip, returning some five months later due to Madeleine's pregnancy.

They boarded Titanic at Southampton on April 10, 1912 and on the night of April 14th Astor was lost in the sinking.

Astor's body was recovered from the sea several days later and was only identifiable by the jacket he wore bearing his initials "JJA" and certain jewelry found on his body. His remains were transported first to Halifax, then to Rhinebeck, New York where he was interred in a very public funeral. *(public domain)*

MADELEINE
FORCE
ASTOR

Following the sinking Madeleine returned to Aiken with her last known visit to be in 1916. In that same year she married William Karl Dick, Vice-President of Manufacturer's Trust Company. She had 2 sons with Dick before their divorce in 1933. She later married Italian prize fighter Enzo Fiermonte and the marriage lasted 5 years. Madeleine died of heart failure in Palm Beach on March 27, 1940 at the age of 46. *(public domain)*

Major Archibald W. Butt, Military Attache to President William H. Taft was a native of Augusta, Georgia and was friends with many Aiken winter colonists. He was returning from a European vacation and visit with Pope Pius X to whom he delivered a letter from the President when he boarded Titanic at Southhampton.

Taft thought of Butt as a son and was deeply affected by his loss, and threw his influence behind several memorial initiatives including the memorial bridge in Augusta.

Butt's body was never recovered from the sea. *(public domain)*

On the night of April 14th George Widener and his wife Eleanor hosted what would become the final dinner honoring Titanic's Captain Smith who would retire following this voyage.
A prominent Phildelphian, Widener continued the business created by his father who had become wealthy in the streetcar business in Philadelphia.
Widener was lost on the night of the sinking. His body, if recovered was unidentifiable. *(public domain)*

Following the sinking, Eleanor Widener, who lost both her husband and 27 year old son Harry, devoted her time to creating a memorial to Harry with the building of the Harry Elkins Widener Library on the campus of Harvard University. At the library's dedication in 1915 she made the acquaintance of Dr. Alexander Rice who she was to marry before the year ended. She spent the rest of her life traveling the world with Rice, as he was an avid explorer. She died of a heart attack in Paris in 1937. (public domain)

Harry Widener was 27 years of age when he went down with Titanic. A collector of rare books, he had been in London and purchased a 1598 edition of Sir Francis Bacon's *Essaies* which he carried on his person at the time of the sinking. Before leaving London he jokingly said to the bookseller, "If I am shipwrecked you will know that this will be on me." Indeed it was in his pocket when Titanic slipped to the bottom of the sea. *(public domain)*

Born in Aiken on February 11, 1900, Tommy Hitchcock, Jr. was 17 years of age when he entered the Lafayette Flying Corps and became a "pilote de chasse" in France's WWI air war against Germany.

With already two "kills" to his credit and going for a third, he was shot down by a German Albatross and taken as a prisoner of war. His daring escape from a prisoner troop train and cross-country trek to neutral Switzerland brought him instant fame in French and American newspapers. The French awarded him the "Croix de Guerre" for his service to France.

(public domain)

The 1920s and '30s were the Tommy Hitchcock years in polo, just as there were Babe Ruth years in baseball, and Bobby Jones years in golf. He carried a 10 goal handicap, the highest ranking in polo. He led 4 teams to the U. S. National Open Polo Championship in 1923, 1927, 1935 and 1936. As a polo celebrity, he was admired by literary figures, Hollywood actors, columnists, business and financial leaders.
(photo courtesy of Aiken Standard)

"Hopelands" was the name given to the Iselin's Aiken winter home on Whiskey Road. Although they were married in 1894, the land was a wedding gift from Col. William Goddard to his daughter and son-in-law in 1897.

The property included stables as Mrs. Iselin was an avid horsewoman.

She died in 1970 at the age of 102. Her estate was bequethed to the City of Aiken to be used as a public park.

(courtesy of Aiken County Historical Museum)

The C. Oliver Iselin family at their Aiken estate, *"Hopelands."* Pictured here with her only surviving child, Hope, at about the age of 5 or 6 (1912-1913) and her favorite dogs, Mrs. Iselin was always a model of modesty despite coming from a family of great wealth.

A prominent yachtsman, C. Oliver successfully defended America's Cup six times; his last defense in 1903.

Oliver and Hope were the driving force supporting the building of Aiken's first hospital in 1917.

(Courtesy of Lisa Hall, Aiken Thoroughbred Racing Hall of Fame)

Aiken's first hospital was located on land donated by the city. The property was originally part of Eustis Park given to the city by Celestine Eustis. The hospital's official name was Aiken Hospital and Relief Society and was opened on May 17, 1917. In 1936, on the same site, it was replaced by a new structure - Aiken County Hospital. *(courtesy of Aiken County Historical Museum)*

West view of the
Highland Park Hotel
following the addition
of the new wing in
1875. *(courtesy of
Allen Riddick)*

Many guests enjoyed the
leisurely relaxation afforded
by the porch system that
embraced the hotel.
It also served as a social
gathering place for societal
guests to chat and intermingle.
(courtesy of Allen Riddick)

The morning of destruction.
Smoke can clearly be seen
billowing from the "L"
junction of the hotel, the
location of the hotel laundry,
and the kitchen located on
the floor above.
*(courtesy of the Aiken
County Historical Museum)*

Nicholas Longworth and "Princess" Alice Roosevelt on their wedding day at the White House, February 17, 1906. The newlyweds are here pictured with Alice's father, President Theodore Roosevelt.

She was beloved by the press and often took center stage.

Their honeymoon began with a visit to "Friendship," Evalyn Walsh McLean's estate in Washington, D.C. McLean was also an Aiken winter colonist.

(public domain)

Pictured here in the later years of their marriage, Alice and Nicholas Longworth had grown somewhat apart. In 1912 Nicholas supported William Howard Taft, from Nicholas's home state, for the Republican Presidential nomination over Alice's father, an event that instigated a rift which would continue to grow between the couple over the years. Nicholas's drinking and womanizing contributed to the couple's problems, and continued until his death in Aiken on April 9th 1931. *(public domain)*

Aiken winter colonist and polo enthusiast, William E. Carter was labeled a coward and given the nickname "Titanic Bill" by the press for dressing like a woman to escape the sinking Titanic, a charge that was never substantiated by the Senate Board of Inquiry. There is evidence that Carter continued to spend winters in Aiken following his 1914 divorce from Lucille Polk Carter. He would also visit Palm Beach where he became a regular guest at Flagler's "The Breakers" Hotel. He died there in 1940. *(public domain)*

Lucille Polk Carter was a descendant of President James K. Polk. She married the wealthy William Ernest Carter in 1896 and divorced him in 1914. The divorce was partially attributed to her husband's behavior during the sinking of Titanic. In 1914 she married George Brooke, Jr., a wealthy banker and steel manufacturer.

Lucille was an avid horsewoman and reportedly was the first woman to play polo astride, and the first woman to drive a four-in-hand.

She died of a heart attack on October 26, 1934 aged 59.
(public domain)

In this rare 1897 photo is Frederick Beach relaxing at Aiken's Palmetto Golf Club. During the winter of 1912 he leased the Turner cottage located next door to his own at Hood's Lane & Newberry Street, which was to become the scene of a grisly crime the night of February 26, 1912. *(courtesy of Allen Riddick)*

Mrs. Camilla Beach *(center)* began coming to Aiken with her first husband, Charles Havemeyer of the Havemeyer Sugar Trust of Wall Street. A horsewoman, she continued coming to Aiken after her marriage to Frederick Beach. The night of February 26, 1912 her throat was slit in the yard of the home they rented, and her husband was indicted for the crime. She was steadfast in her claim that an unknown negro was the perpetrator despite strong circumstantial evidence suggesting a crime of passion. *(public domain)*

Mayor Herbert Gyles served two terms as Mayor of Aiken. He was the force in ensuring that the Beach investigation would continue to its final outcome by leading City Council to hire M.S. Baughn, an outsider, to investigate the crime.

In addition to serving as Mayor, Gyles served two terms as State Representative. He was a lawyer and in later years moved to Washington, D.C. where he accepted a post in the federal government.

(public domain)

Beach hired Col. Daniel Henderson as Chief Counsel to lead his sizeable defense team consisting of local as well as Wall Street lawyers.

At the time, Henderson was the Dean of the Aiken Bar, a prestigious title which inferred significant influence as well as top legal talent.

Earlier, Henderson had been a State Senator from Aiken during the 1880s.

He was highly respected in Aiken and the State throughout his life.

(public domain)

Hood's Lane viewed from its corner with Newberry St. The laundry building was located inside the larger gate entry *(right)*. Beyond the far column is Beach's home *(out of view)*, but on 2/26/12 he was leasing the corner home.
(author's collection)

TITANIC BILL

Every aristocratic gentleman knows what is expected of him at all times. It is no less true than in times of great stress and crisis. It is an unwritten code which is bred into him at conception, and emphasized throughout the blossoming of every upper-class Anglo-Saxon gentleman.

First and foremost, always defend the honor and safety of a lady. Secondly, bear any hardship with a stiff upper lip, and do whatever is necessary, even under the most difficult of circumstances, to preserve civility and the family's good name and reputation.

This unwritten code was the true litmus test for the aristocratic men occupying the first-class cabins on the White Star Line's *Titanic* at two o'clock on the morning of April 15, 1912. A number of Aiken's winter colonists—John Jacob Astor IV, George Widener, Harry Widener, James Clinch Smith, and Archibald Butt—met that test at the cost of their lives. One other did not.

Whether millionaire William Ernest Carter, of Philadelphia and Aiken, passed that test was much debated in the official inquiry, newspaper reports, and society social gossip following the disaster at sea. Many said he did not, earning him the epithet "Titanic Bill," a dubious title, quite unfit for a gentleman, which followed him for the rest of his life.

Carter's crime was surviving *Titanic's* sinking along with White Star Line's managing director, Bruce Ismay, both of whom dashed into collapsible lifeboat "C" at the moment it was swung over the side for lowering, defying the continuously shouted order: "Women only in the lifeboats." Further magnifying Carter's felony was the fact that, in addition to adult males not being allowed, some male children were not allowed into the lifeboats, resulting in numerous male children losing their lives.

Born on June 19, 1875, William Ernest Carter was the son of William Thornton Carter and Cornelia Redington Carter. His father achieved vast wealth owning and operating his coal mines in Carbon County, Pennsylvania, which allowed young William to grow up in a privileged environment, permitting him to focus on what he loved best—polo.

Perhaps growing up in comfort and luxury, never needing to be gainfully employed, and having a coterie of servants answering every whim and desire had impacted William's character and ability to make difficult life decisions. Although his shipboard peers had matured within the same environmental and familial conditions, they did meet the ultimate test with grace.

Carter was thirty-six years old at the time of the sinking, and certainly at that point in his life he should have internalized the "unwritten code" required of all upper-class gentlemen, but some would say he did not. Some perhaps would argue that he had been genetically flawed at birth, something that could have remained hidden for his entire life absent a crisis like the one presented on the night of April 14–15, 1912. Or, for some reason associated with psyche, he could not bring himself to do his duty. In any case, once all was revealed by the board of inquiry, it was easier for the general public to label him a "coward" and shout a slogan, "Titanic Bill," each time he was seen in public or spoken about.

It clearly bothered Carter to be an upper-class male survivor of the sinking, because following his testimony during the Senate Board of Inquiry, he refused newspaper interviews or even casual conversation about that fateful night. He just didn't want to talk about it, but it certainly, inexorably, played on his mind.

Carter's refusal to publicly discuss the sequence of events that took place as the disaster unfolded may have contributed to the rumors and stories that developed, further denigrating his character and reputation. If he had permitted interviews, perhaps he could have ameliorated the perception to a certain degree or even exonerated himself.

One story that gained prominence and received vigorous circulation was that Carter, dressed as a woman, used his disguise to secure a seat in a lifeboat. The general public, not wanting to be bothered by reading many monotonous lines of testimony taken by the Board of Inquiry, some of which ran counter to this tale, eagerly adopted the cross-dress story, which gave rise to the "Titanic Bill" label. The flames of their eagerness were fanned by a press seeking as much sensationalism as possible, adding distortion to the greatest non-wartime maritime tragedy in history.

Aiken, South Carolina
Winter 1912

Upon arrival at Aiken's train depot, and while disembarking his railroad car, William Carter was once again reminded of his "crime" as young boys loitering near the loading ramp who recognized him from newspaper sketches began shouting, "Hey, Titanic Bill, where's your dress?" It had only been eight months since the disaster at sea, but it seemed an eternity as Carter once again turned a deaf ear to the taunts he had heard so many times before in Philadelphia and his hometown, Unionville, Pennsylvania.

He and his wife, Lucille Polk Carter,[112] quietly settled into their perennial rental, the Clinkscale's cottage[113] on Hayne Avenue, where they planned to spend a quiet winter enjoying the mild Aiken climate.

Lucille and her husband's relationship changed for the worse following the disaster at sea. Some of it attributable to the withering fire of insults verbally hurled at them in public, some for the way he comported himself on the night of, and the following morning of the tragedy. Lucille was unaccustomed to this type of behavior and anything short of courtly manners.

I won't be competing this season in the sport that I love, but will quietly

---

112 A descendant of President James K. Polk, Lucille Polk Carter was born in Baltimore in 1875 to Louisa and William Polk. Polk was a partner in the very successful insurance brokerage firm Hopper, Polk & Purnell of Baltimore. She married Clark in 1896 at the age of twenty-one.

113 The Clinkscale cottage is located next door to a home that would, in later years, be owned by local businessman George Durban and his wife, Rosa.

recuperate from the injury I sustained in the Bryn Mawr – Philadelphia Country Club Polo Match[114] this past June, thought William Carter.

During the first few weeks, Carter regularly visited Whitney Field, but now as a spectator instead of a participant. He understood the seriousness of his injury, and was not about to jeopardize his recovery by jumping onto the back of a polo pony. He would sometimes visit the Palmetto Golf Club to see old friends and visit with George Widener, Jr.,[115] who was also passing the season in Aiken with his beloved thoroughbreds. George would often ask about his father and brother's last minutes, as they were with Carter onboard *Titanic*, and were lost in the sinking.

One evening while he and Lucille were ensconced in the overstuffed chairs of the Clinkscale's study absorbed in their reading, which was their habit following their evening meal, William's mind played the railroad depot boys' taunts over and over, still ringing in his ears, raising mental havoc, and he desperately wanted to do something about it.

"Lucille, do you think I did the right thing?" he asked, as he dropped his book, removed his spectacles, and looked up to his wife with a plaintive expression on his face.

Without another word of explanation, she knew exactly what was on his mind.

"William, if you're asking for my advice, I can say that I think your silence since the sinking has encouraged the entire world to run roughshod over your reputation and dignity as a man. You have never asked me about this since that awful night, and I have been reluctant to interfere with your thoughts, but while it may be a bit late to offer a public defense, it would be better than what you've allowed the public to do thus far," she said in a most serious tone.

"Well, it is clear that the masses are content to take on the newspaper stories as truth and ignore the record and my own testimony before

---

114   Carter sustained shock and a concussion after landing on his shoulder and the side of his head in a fall when his polo pony buckled, fell, and rolled over him in June 1912 while competing in the Goughacres Polo Cup.

115   Widener's father and brother both went down with *Titanic*. The Widener and Carter families were fellow Philadelphians and friends.

the Board of Inquiry. And as it certainly seems today, that will never change unless I take some sort of action. As you also know, our invitations from friends and acquaintances have fallen off, so I would suspect that the vitriol has crept into our personal world as well," he said with an increasing level of annoyance in his voice.

"Just look at what the reporters did to poor old Sloper,"[116] he continued. "Because he wouldn't give them an interview, they described him in their story as *the man who got off dressed like a woman*. A total lie, and now the poor devil is forever defending himself."

"I will need to tell the story from top to bottom in order to have any chance of stopping the gossip," he added as his mind began a pensive search into the memory of eight months prior…

Lucille and the children[117] had just returned to first-class cabins B-96 and 98 from the sumptuous dinner hosted by George and Eleanor Widener in honor of *Titanic's* Captain Smith. I remained behind to enjoy a cigar, brandy, and play some cards with Major Archibald Butt, Harry Widener, and Clarence Moore.[118]

The ocean was like glass, and one could hardly detect any movement at all. Not even the brandy stirred as it settled into our crystal Waterfords.

By 11:40 p.m. we had only played a few hands before our peace was broken by a shudder followed by vibrations coming from the starboard forward half of the ship. My fellow card players looked at one another questioningly. Major Butt was first to react as he abruptly left the table and went out to the starboard deck. He returned moments later with a large chunk of ice in his hands.

---

116   William Sloper of New Britain, CT, legitimately left *Titanic* in lifeboat #7, the first to be lowered. Ship's officers were allowing anyone to leave in a lifeboat at that time as no one believed the ship was in serious danger during first warnings, so there were few takers as they tried unsuccessfully to fill the lifeboats. There is no evidence supporting the statement that Sloper was dressed as a woman, despite *The New York Journal's* story accusing him of such.

117   Carter's eleven-year-old son, William, and his seven-year-old daughter, Lucille, accompanied the couple on *Titanic* along with two domestic staff.

118   Maj. Butt was military attaché to President Taft. Widener was the son of George and Eleanor Widener. Clarence Moore was a wealthy clubman from Maryland who had gone to England to purchase fox hounds.

"Gentlemen, it appears that we have struck an iceberg. Would anyone be needing ice for your drink?" he said as he held up a sizable piece of glacier.

In fact, three hundred feet of deck were littered with chunks of broken glacier. The major had arrived on the deck in time to see a towering iceberg, extending an additional thirty feet above the boat deck, pass by and disappear into the watery darkness.

While my fellow card players were somewhat unfazed by our experience, which was reinforced by passing ship's stewards who calmly assured us that the engines, which were now stopped, was surely a temporary incident. I left the table and headed for my staterooms to check on Lucille and the children.[119]

On my route to the room, I saw passengers trickling out onto the passageways in various states of dress, walking and stumbling over the many chunks of broken ice, asking questions of one another and any passing ship's personnel as to what was happening. I knew at this moment that the situation was more than just a temporary incident as I could already detect a slight listing of the ship to port. I was determined to do what was necessary to protect my family.

"Lucille, children, you must get dressed now as the ship has had an accident," I said, trying to maintain a calm demeanor.

At that same moment, a gentle knock came to the stateroom door, and a very composed ship's steward asked us to kindly dress warmly, put on our life jackets, and come up to the boat deck as soon as possible. He stressed that this was just a precaution. I suspected that this was something being told to all passengers in order to avoid a panic.

"You can be honest with us—just how serious a problem do you think it is?" Lucille asked the steward. "My husband has seen chunks of glacier ice on the outer passageways."

"Madam, we have struck an iceberg, and our lower compartments are taking on water. I would recommend you all dress warmly and proceed to the boat deck as soon as possible. I'm sorry," he returned as he

---

119   The Carter party also included Carter's manservant, Lucille's maid, and the family's chauffer, who were all quartered in the second-class portion of the ship.

calmly left for the next stateroom.

By the time Lucille and I had the children dressed and prepared, it was well past midnight when we started for "A" deck. On arrival I could see that several boats had already been launched, and men were milling around in the frigid cold, stamping their feet to stay warm. Women and girls only were allowed into the boats. No men or male children allowed. Such was the captain's order. I immediately thought of young William, who stood by my side as lifeboat #4 was loading.

Second Ship's Officer Charles Lightoller was in charge of loading lifeboat #4 on "A" Deck. As he helped ladies into the boat, he kept a Johnny Bull's stern eye on the men who were standing close. I was standing with dear friend George Widener and his son, Harry. They were fellow Philadelphians, and George was helping his wife, Eleanor, and her maid into the boat. John Jacob Astor was standing nearby, who, after seeing his new wife, Madeleine, into the boat, remained in hopes that his request to accompany her due to her "delicate" condition would be granted.

"Lucille, take my hand, as you must now get into the boat. You will be with Eleanor, so it will be all right," I said, and I turned to my eleven-year-old son.

"Mr. Lightoller, please allow the boy to accompany his mother. He is only eleven years old and should be given a chance," I pled while taking young William by the arm to help him board.

"Only women and girls allowed in the lifeboats, sir," shot back Lightoller.

What quickly followed next was totally unexpected!

"There—now he is a girl, so let him in with his mother!" said John Jacob Astor as he placed a lady's hat on young William's head.[120]

Completely taken aback by Astor's firm and riveting stare, one that I'm sure he's used many times in business transactions, Lightoller stood with mouth agape while Astor helped the boy into the boat, all the while meeting with unblinking eyes Lightoller's stare.

---

120 Accounts differ on who placed the ladies' hat on young William. The legend has grown around Astor doing so, but it is also stated that Mrs. Carter placed her hat on the boy.

I have no idea where Astor obtained the lady's hat, but there it was now sitting on young William's head as he settled into the boat beside his mother.

"Lower away," shouted Lightoller, and deck hands swung the lifeboat out into the cold night air away and down *Titanic's* giant flank.

I remained on the deck watching, along with the others, as our families were lowered into the freezing black water below.

Astor, myself, George and Harry Widener, and Archibald Butt, who had recently joined our huddle, remained on the boat deck and began to speculate on our situation, which appeared dire.

"Thank you, Colonel,"[121] I said to Astor. "You have probably saved young William's life."

"It's quite all right, Carter. Well, what do you think, will we be seeing one another in Aiken next season?" he asked rhetorically, with what I could detect was a bit of doubt in his voice.

"Will any of you be trying for a boat?" I asked no one in particular in our group of men.

"I'll take my chances here on the big ship," responded Harry Widener, while the others remained silent, some puffing cigars, others breathing on their hands in an effort to keep them warm.

I bid my friends good-bye and walked among the throngs that were once civil passengers, but now were a mob near panic, as the ocean had climbed to within ten feet of the boat deck. Some were rushing to the stern as it rose from the ocean's surface; others sought out the very few lifeboats available; and others, mostly foreigners in steerage, were jumping from the rail into the freezing water below.

I crossed over from the port side, where lifeboats #2, 4, 6, and 8 were being launched, to the starboard, where boats #1, 3, 5, 7 were now gone. The remaining eight boats were stored aft and were almost all gone as well. Onboard *Titanic*, in addition to sixteen lifeboats, were four collapsible lifeboats, so identified as A, B, C, and D. These had wooden bottoms and canvas sides. They were stored upside down with

---

121 Astor preferred to be called either "Jack" by his close friends and family, or "Colonel" by others—a title he was given during his involvement in the Spanish-American War of 1898.

the sides folded in and would need to be erected and placed on davits in order to be used. By 1:45 a.m. nearly all of the lifeboats had been launched and the collapsibles were being righted for launching.

I saw Bruce Ismay, managing director of White Star Lines, standing near collapsible lifeboat C, and I went over to join him. Chief Officer Wilde was in charge of collapsible C and he, along with Ismay, were now shouting for women and children to board. I noticed that Officer Wilde was holding a pistol in his right hand as a warning to any man trying to board. Just prior to my arrival, he and Ship's Quartermaster George Rowe had finished pulling men out of the collapsible by their ankles, throwing them to the deck. The brandished pistol was meant to be a deterrent to any other males thinking of boarding collapsible C.

I joined in with Ismay in shouting for any women and children to present themselves for boarding as there were still many vacant seats in the lifeboat. There were approximately forty passengers in the boat, mostly females from "Steerage Class," and the boat's capacity was sixty-five. There were no women or children to be seen anywhere on our part of the deck.

Since there were seats available, I asked if I could join the women as there were none remaining to fill the boat. I received no answer to my question.

"We cannot tarry any longer. Lower away!" shouted Chief Officer Wilde to the crewmen manning the ropes.

As the lifeboat was about to be swung over the side, Ismay leaped in, and in the blink of an eye I followed, not caring if Wilde fired his pistol or not, for I clearly knew that *Titanic* would soon be at the bottom of the ocean.

Such a small event—a two-second leap into a boat—would take months or perhaps stretch into years of explanation, thanks to the voracious appetite for drama and sensationalism held by so many news reporters. Never did I think that my decision to survive would be so maligned.

After floating aimlessly for what seemed an eternity in the collapsible lifeboat, which had taken on water and froze our feet and legs, we could see dawn begin to break in the east. We now saw many large, blue-tinged icebergs floating nearby, and we also saw the now quiet and lifeless bodies of men, women, and children being kept afloat by cork-filled life jackets bobbing in the nearly calm water. Many had faces still contorted by the last moments of anguished desperation and agony. In the distance we could see a steamer heading our way, and we were instantly uplifted at the prospect of a rescue.

"William, William," Lucille calmly called as she removed her spectacles and put down her book, breaking her husband's near trance state. "William, I want you to remain civil and calm as I tell you what has been on my mind for some time. Your version of what happened on the ship differs with what I remember from that night, as your behavior did not reflect well on your honor as a gentleman, but more importantly, on your concern for family," she said very seriously.

"Disappearing into the crowd, you all but abandoned us on the boat deck that night, and young William would have remained there with the men had I not put my hat on his head and passed him as a girl," she said with a voice now beginning to rise with anger. "When we boarded the lifeboat, you were nowhere to be found. After daybreak, when we arrived on the rescue ship *Carpathia*, you were already there, and I will never forget your smug comment to us as we boarded. 'I didn't think you would make it' was a most inappropriate and hateful greeting on first seeing your family after narrowly escaping a dreadful fate," she added with rising anger.

"Your actions that night were despicably revealing, and have led our relationship to become increasingly distant since last April—distant enough that I can now tell you that I have sought legal advice, and directed my attorney to file for divorce," she finished, now somewhat relieved that her up-until-then secret plan had been divulged.

"William, please have our railcar ready to leave the Aiken depot, as I plan to return to Philadelphia tomorrow. I hope you will honor my request as a gentleman," she said, her voice now returning to a calm and quiet timbre.

"But Lucille, Lucille, can't we talk about this?" William asked in desperation.

Without acknowledgment or answer, Lucille Polk Carter calmly rose from her chair, book in hand, and retired to her bedroom to pack for the morning departure for Philadelphia.

THE REST OF THE STORY

Lucille Polk Carter did in fact obtain a divorce from William Carter in January[122] of 1914. Included in the decree, her version of William's behavior aboard the *Titanic* was recounted as part of her argument and subsequently became grist for the societal gossip mill.

Lucille continued to take part in society activities and was considered *avant garde* by her peers. She had somewhat of a reputation of being an iconoclast when it came to acceptable, traditional fashion while attending society's many elegant events, including equestrian as she was an avid horsewoman and loved polo.

During her marriage, she and William not only came to Aiken, but also traveled the Newport and Europe societal circuit as well.

On August 16, 1914, Lucille married George Brooke, a wealthy Philadelphia banker and steel manufacturer, in a secret London ceremony. The following month they sailed back to Pennsylvania aboard the *Olympic, Titanic's* sister ship!

Lucille Polk Carter Brooke died at Ithan, Pennsylvania, on October 26, 1934 following a heart attack. She was fifty-nine years of age.

William Ernest Carter's account of the events onboard *Titanic* during the sinking were at odds with the findings of the Board of Inquiry, based on the testimony of others. Curiously, during his testimony

---

122   Alternate sources cite spring of 1914 as the divorce date.

before the Board, Carter praised the actions of Bruce Ismay, White Star's managing director.

Interestingly, in the 1997 movie production *Titanic*, there was a sequence where the lead characters took refuge in an automobile located in *Titanic's* cargo hold. Following the disaster, Carter lodged a $5,000 claim with White Star Line for the loss of a new, forty-six horsepower Renault he had purchased in France that he was transporting to the U.S., presumably the same one depicted in the movie.

Based on newspaper reports, Carter possessed an unsympathetic, terse, condescending personality, and could be rude, particularly when interacting with individuals outside his social class.

Following the revelations associated with the divorce, he became somewhat of an outsider as his wife's allegations became known to his peers. Perhaps this was his punishment for violating the "Gentlemen's Code" on that fateful night.

In later years he continued venturing from his country estate, Gwenda Farm, located in Unionville, Pennsylvania, to visit Aiken, but also developed a liking for the luxury hotel built by Henry Flagler in Palm Beach, The Breakers, where he became a regular guest.

While he was a guest at The Breakers, Carter became ill and was taken to Good Samaritan Hospital in West Palm Beach, where he died on Wednesday, March 20, 1940.

AIKEN'S TRIAL
OF THE CENTURY

It had been since 1905, when millionaire Frederick O. Beach purchased the Allison Cottage on the corner of Laurens Street and Hood Lane from Mrs. T. G. Croft, that he and his socialite wife, Camilla Woodward Moss Havemeyer, had been spending winters in Aiken. But on a mild February night in 1912, their world of social gentility would be violently shaken following a most villainous and bloody occurrence that took place outside their serene Aiken winter home.

Frederick O. Beach cut a handsome, sophisticated figure as a well-known, sought-after man-about-town. He attended the best primary and secondary schools, and was a graduate of Yale. During his business career he was a partner in the New York stock brokerage firm of Tailer & Robinson. The stock market and other business ventures he was associated with had made him very wealthy, to the point where, as a relatively young man, he was able to devote all his time pursuing his favorite hobbies, polo and coach driving. When in Aiken he divided his time between the polo field, the Palmetto Golf Club, and the Tennis Club. When in New York he was regularly seen at the most exclusive clubs, including the Metropolitan, Meadow Brook Hunt, Knickerbocker, and other clubs frequented by the elite. His circle of friends came from the highest perches of New York society. William K. Vanderbilt was his best man on the day he married Camilla Havemeyer, and he was a frequent guest aboard the Vanderbilt yacht. It was said that he became engaged with Camilla after meeting her aboard Vanderbilt's yacht during the summer before their November 1899 wedding. Also numbered among his friends were: Philadelphia railroad and investment millionaire Clarence Dolan; wealthy New York lawyer Winthrop Rutherfurd; C. Oliver Iselin, America's Cup yachtsman and investment banking heir; and Thomas Hitchcock, all of whom were also members of Aiken's winter colony.

Camilla Moss was the daughter of Courtlandt Moss, a banker associated with The Central National Bank of the City of New York. She has been described as high spirited, beautiful, and a top-ranked horsewoman. She was a member of the Meadow Brook Club on Long Island, where she was a frequent participant in equestrian events. It was during one such equine outing that she caught the attention of Charles F. Havemeyer, who was also an equine devotee and grandson of Frederick Havemeyer, founder of the sugar trust, Havemeyer and Elder of Wall Street in New York City. In 1890, Camilla became Mrs. Charles F. Havemeyer, a match that was not well accepted by the Havemeyer family, as Camilla was not of similar societal rank. For a number of years, Camilla and "Carley," as Charles was called, wintered in Aiken, and along with other winter colonists enjoyed the fox hunts, polo, and other social activities throughout the winter months.

It was rumored that by the third year of their marriage, unhappiness had settled into their relationship, and in 1897, it was reported that Charles left her for a time, but was later reconciled through the efforts of a family member.

On Monday evening, May 10, 1898, the family was preparing to receive evening dinner guests at their Roslyn, New York, home. Havemeyer went upstairs, presumably to his bedroom for a change of clothes. Moments later a pistol shot was heard coming from his study. Camilla, responding to the loud report, immediately ran to her husband's room to find him sitting in his chair, arm outstretched with a .32 caliber pistol still in hand, and a bullet hole in his head. The family doctor was called, but Havemeyer was already dead on his arrival. The coroner ruled the incident an accidental death, and it was politely theorized that Mr. Havemeyer was shot while cleaning his loaded pistol.

Camilla was now heir to Havemeyer millions!

During the summer of 1899, as a guest aboard William Vanderbilt's yacht, Camilla was introduced to Frederick O. Beach. The two were immediately drawn to one another, she a beautiful, wealthy heiress, and he a handsome,[123] wealthy businessman who shared her love of equine sports. They began a relationship, and on November 28 of that same year were married at Grace Episcopal Church in New York City. Camilla had already been an Aiken winter visitor; now Frederick joined her in winter activities in the "Newport of the South."

Although known as a jovial, well-adjusted fellow, Beach possessed a jealous streak, as it was reported. Perhaps this was his fatal flaw, or perhaps he was misjudged. His wife, a high-spirited, desirable woman who attended many societal gatherings, no doubt caught the attention of many men who may have held private thoughts of unspeakable desires…

Aiken, South Carolina
Monday, February 26, 1912
9:30 p.m.

Camilla Beach and her husband Frederick were relaxing in the reading room and were about to retire for the evening. Camilla's house guest, Miss Marion Hollins,[124] daughter of Harry B. Hollins of the New York banking and brokerage firm H. B. Hollins & Company, had already gone to the upstairs guest bedroom.

This particular season, Camilla, Frederick, and the Beaches' maid, Pearl Hampton, were occupying the Turner cottage located on the corner of Hood's Lane and Newberry Street, next door to their own winter home, which they had leased for the season to Mr. J. D. Lyon of Pittsburgh. The properties were separated by a pathway and the

---

123 Beach was known as "Beauty Beach" by eligible society women of the time. For that reason and for his wealth, he was considered a highly desirable catch.

124 Marion Hollins was the U.S. Women's Amateur Golf Champion in 1921, and captain of the U.S. Curtis Cup team in 1932. As a golf course designer, she had worked with Alister MacKenzie to design Cypress Point and Pasatiempo Golf Clubs. She was the reason Bobby Jones hired MacKenzie to design Augusta National.

Beaches' laundry, a small building that stood in the side yard of their home. Surrounding the home was a white picket fence with a hedge border. The Beaches' neighbor, Dr. Hastings Wyman, a local doctor and an Aiken city councilman, lived directly across Newberry Street.

As she was preparing to go outside to give her dogs an airing, Camilla thought she heard her name being called from somewhere out in the yard.

"Mrs. Beach, Mrs. Beach, I have a message for you from Katie.[125] Mrs. Beach, come out and I will give it to you," came the raspy, subdued voice calling from the top of the walkway near the picket fence gate.

The voice easily carried through the screened door as the evening was mild and the inner door was left open to allow the cool evening breeze to enter. The maid, Pearl Hampton, had been out and was, at that time, on her way back to the Beach home.

"Yes, this is Mrs. Beach. What do you want?" said Camilla with some trepidation as she approached the screened door, trying to discern the male figure standing at the top of the yard's walkway.

"Come out, Mrs. Beach, I have a note for you from Katie. Come out and I will give it to you," the hissing, raspy voice replied.

With her dog in tow, Camilla stepped out and began heading toward the dark figure awaiting her near the gate. It was a bright moonlit night, and as she approached she saw that it was a large Negro man wearing an overcoat and waving a note in his outstretched right hand. She could not see his other hand as he held it behind his back.

As she approached and reached to take the note, he swiftly pulled his hand back and, with his left, swung an already bloodied fence paling, striking Camilla's head. Stunned, she could not struggle, and in almost a single motion, he quickly grabbed her from behind. Locking his left arm around her upper chest, with his right hand he thrust a knife blade into the left side of her throat, ripping across its front and letting loose a wave of blood which copiously poured as it followed the

---

125   The reference was to Camilla's friend Katie Smith, who was a guest at the Joseph Harriman cottage.

knife's trace to the opposite side of her neck.

The piercing pain and shock of the knife's sinking into her neck immediately brought from Camilla a loud and terrific scream that could be heard throughout the quiet neighborhood. On her second scream, now heard more as a gurgled yelp, Frederick was roused from his chair and was on his way in a dash out the door. Camilla's assailant, in a brutal swipe, ripped off her earrings and fled upon seeing Frederick running down the walkway.

Seeing his wife covered in blood, Frederick, who initially began to chase the assailant, returned to render aid. As he lifted her into his arms, blood continued to ooze, and with each agitation as Camilla grew hysterical, blood would flow in a pulsating gush that now covered his arms, shirt, and trousers in warm, sticky crimson as he hurriedly carried her into the home.

Responding to the screams heard throughout the neighborhood and Frederick's frantic knocking on his front door, the Beaches' neighbor, Dr. Wyman, was first on the scene with medical aid. After an emergency assessment that the penetration had not been deep enough to sever vocal cords, and while Frederick did what he could to stanch the flow of blood, Dr. Wyman applied nine stitches, closing the wound. The blow to her head, while painful, did not require any invasive medical attention.

The fence paling that struck Camilla was already bloody because immediately before her attack, the assailant had struck the Beaches' maid, Pearl Hampton, with the same club, and she had almost reached the Beach home.

While the assault on Camilla was taking place, Pearl Hampton was in the process of righting herself from her assault, but was not seriously injured. She was in a position to observe the attack on Camilla and hear the assailant.

A bloody paling, missing from the Beaches' picket fence, was later found in the yard. The motive was thought to be robbery as Camilla's diamond earrings were torn from her ears.

"And that's the story the Beaches gave about the events that took place at their home on the night of February 26th 1912. They stuck to that story throughout the investigation and it was even repeated in court," said M. S. Baughn, special detective hired by the City of Aiken.

Several weeks had passed before Baughn was hired by the city and came to Aiken from Atlanta to work on the case. Several weeks had passed because the Pinkertons were first to investigate the matter, but for reasons unexplained had abandoned the case, giving no special reason for their exit.[126] In a determined effort to resolve the matter, Mayor Herbert E. Gyles, Sr.[127] called an executive session of the Aiken City Council for the purpose of approving the hiring of a special detective. As a result, Baughn was contacted and hired because of his experience and role in collecting evidence used in the highly publicized conviction of "Abe" Ruef, the confessed San Francisco grafter.[128]

Baughn reported directly to Mayor Gyles, who had now taken an active part in the investigation.

Immediately after his hiring, Baughn interviewed a number of individuals, including the Beaches, Pearl Hampton, Miss Marion Hollins, Dr. Marion Wyman, Mrs. Marion Wyman, Dr. Hastings Wyman, Sr., and Lallah Wyman, who had heard Camilla's screams and came out her door quickly enough to see a "man in a gray suit" flee the scene. Marion Hollins, also reacting to the screams, dashed out onto the upstairs balcony adjoining her bedroom, heard voices, and also saw a "man in a gray suit" fleeing the area. He also interviewed Sheriff H. H. Howard and Officer S. E. Holley, who was the first policeman on the scene the

---

126 Reportedly, some speculated that the Pinkerton investigation was a "whitewash" because of the societal level of the people involved. Further speculating—this could be due to the fact that a Pinkerton heir having substantial control in the family's detective agency was also a winter colonist in Aiken, and certainly knew the parties involved.

127 Gyles served two terms as mayor and two terms as a state representative. He was a charter member of the Aiken Rotary Club.

128 Ruef was head of a powerful but corrupt San Francisco political machine. He was tried and convicted of bribing city supervisors and was sentenced to fourteen years in San Quentin Prison in 1907–08.

night of the attack.

Up until the time of Baughn's arrival, many aspects of the investigation were inconclusive enough that no arrest had been made, and in fact, the Beaches continued to stay at their leased winter cottage until March 25th when they left for New York, where they would board a transatlantic liner and depart for a London vacation with the William Vanderbilts.

Prior to Beach's indictment, rumors flew and speculative newspaper articles began to appear, causing a number of winter colonist friends to come to his defense. In particular, Mr. C. Oliver Iselin, in a letter addressed to Mayor Gyles, stated that he would take pleasure in participating in a lynching of persons spreading gossip about the Beaches. Additionally, Iselin offered a reward for the capture of the guilty person or persons.

Iselin wrote, "I sincerely trust these rewards[129] and those which will be offered by others may bring about the results we all hope for, and will also help to run to earth the scandalmongers whose foul tongues have maliciously attached the good name of one who already, by the most undoubted testimony, has been proved to be above slightest suspicion."

He further wrote, "I consider myself a law-abiding citizen, but it would give me much pleasure to participate in the lynching of the person or persons who are responsible for such slanderous accusations."

As a result of Baughn's investigative efforts, an arrest warrant was issued on April 8th, and the Aiken County grand jury found a true bill against Beach on June 5th for assault and battery with intent to kill.

The main piece of evidence reviewed by the grand jury, and the most damning, was a pocket knife belonging to Frederick O. Beach, which was acquired by Mayor Gyles,[130] that had been microscopically tested and found to have human blood on one of its blades. Such was Dr. Hastings Wyman's testimony, as it was he who had the knife's blade analyzed, and maintained it in his possession. A main witness, the

---

129   Iselin personally offered a $500 reward in the name of the City of Aiken.

130   It is unclear how Gyles received the knife. One report stated that Beach gave it to him; another suggested that Gyles found it in Beach's yard. Although Beach denied owning a knife, ownership of the knife was certain as Beach's initials were engraved in gold on the knife's casing.

Negro maid Pearl Hampton,[131] who was also attacked the same night as Mrs. Beach, was deemed unreliable following her changing statements about not knowing the identity of her attacker, and ultimately her refusal to answer any questions about the night of the attack.

Beach was at Claridge's Hotel in London when the indictment was handed down, and he was apprised by cable.[132] Calling the charges ridiculous and vowing to clear his name, he sent word that he would be returning to New York immediately and would make himself available for trial in Aiken, when required to do so. His lead attorney, Col. Daniel S. Henderson, posted bond for him with the Aiken County Court of General Sessions.

Frederick Beach lost no time in assembling his defense team. In New York, he engaged the firm of Nicolls, Annable, Lindsay & Fuller, with Mr. Thomas S. Fuller as lead. In Aiken, he retained Col. Daniel Henderson, who was dean of the Aiken Bar, as lawyer-in-charge, with other members of the team consisting of W. Q. Davis, Julian Salley, and Congressman James F. Byrnes, all of Aiken.

The prosecution's team consisted of one person—Second Circuit Solicitor Robert L. Gunter. Gunter knew he was facing formidable legal opponents and requested assistance from Governor Coleman Blease[133] to release part of the state's contingency fund, or for support from a solicitor in another circuit for assistance in prosecuting the case. Although promised, no help was forthcoming. Additionally, as each of the state's witnesses was brought forward to post bond, assuring their appearance in court, Beach's defense attorneys provided the cash for their bonds and immediately whisked them away to the defense's headquarters. Gunter complained about the unfairness of his situation to no avail. Additionally, his lead investigator, M. S. Baughn, his character

---

131 As a Beach-employed domestic servant, it appears she was reluctant to incriminate her employer.

132 When Beach received word of the indictment on April 9, 1912 in London, he inquired about the next liner leaving for America and was told the *Titanic* was leaving on the next day. He reportedly responded, "That's good, I may have to go on her." He later changed his mind and decided to join the Vanderbilts in Paris before leaving for America.

133 Coleman Livingston Blease, born near Newberry, SC, served in the SC House as a protégé of "Pitchfork" Ben Tillman. He later served in the Senate, and in 1910 as mayor of Newberry until elected governor that same year.

impugned through public innuendo, was accused of building a false case in order to collect the reward money (which he was ineligible to receive).

It was very clear that Solicitor Gunter was in for an uphill battle but was relying on two major pieces of evidence:

First, the pocket knife with the bloody blade, belonging to Frederick Beach, that had been found through analysis to have traces of human blood. Dr. Wyman was to testify.

Second, a conversation that was surreptitiously acquired by hiding a newspaper reporter, a Mr. Thompson, in Gunter's office while the Beaches thought they were there alone. The reporter, hiding behind a bookcase, listened in on a conversation between Frederick and Camilla. During that conversation the name "Robert Bronson"[134] surfaced as the couple verbally sparred, and Solicitor Gunter planned to use jealousy as the motive for the attack. It was clear that Solicitor Gunter thought that Bronson was the "man in the gray suit" seen running from the scene by Ms. Wyman and Ms. Hollins.

THE PROSECUTION'S THEORY

In a meeting between M. S. Baughn and Robert Gunter, the two discussed their theory of the case, based on what they believed to be the facts.

"Robert, as you know, I disagree with the Beaches' version of the events of this case. I've given you all that we were able to discover, and I don't think there is much more to learn. Have you made a plan for your presentation?" asked Baughn.

"I have, and I'd like you to listen to be sure we've sequenced correctly

---

134   It is possible that Robert Bronson may have been the son of Frederick Bronson, a wealthy New York, who, like Beach, was a coach-driving aficionado.

what we believe to be the heart of the case," replied Solicitor Gunter.

"On the night of the attack, Beach and wife were seated in the reading room of the Turner Cottage. Mrs. Beach left to put the dog out, remaining out a little long, prompting Beach to step out onto the porch from where he did not see his wife. He walked down the porch to the left side, coming out overlooking the portion of the yard towards the Lyons' home, not seeing anyone. He walked back to the steps and around the path at the corner of his house, going around Newberry Street and out the side gate to the point where the palings were pulled off the fence. Here he had a clear view of the laundry building in the Lyons' lot."

"Remember that we found the paling at the big pool of blood at the side of the house," interjected Baughn.

"Yes, and if it was in Beach's hand, he ran around Hood's Lane and through the big gate and along the hedge, as tracks were found there the next morning made by a size seven or eight shoe, according to Chief Howard. And it was at the end of this hedge, which stops at the walk going from the Lyons' house to the laundry building, that the party came into contact with the Negro maid, Pearl Hampton, who states she was on her way home. But, it is possible that Beach, missing his wife and finding the maid near the yard, presumed that she was communicating with Mrs. Beach. And any undertone voices heard then was Beach's trying to make Pearl tell where Mrs. Beach was. Angered by not receiving what he thought was a truthful answer, he struck her with the fence paling, and this was about the same time as the first scream was heard by the Wymans, who also heard the voices from across the street. Miss Hollins also heard the voices."

"That's right, and that's why Beach ran toward the opening in the partition fence back of the laundry building, to keep from being seen," added Baughn.

"I believe that is so, and as he ran in that direction, going through the opening of the partition fence at the Lyons' lot, a man in a neat gray suit ran out of the big gate in the Lyons' lot. It was only about three or four minutes after the gray-suited man ran out that the next screams were heard in the Turner lot, the Beaches' rental. This would have given Beach time to run back through the partition fence and catch Mrs. Beach at the place where the first pool of blood was found. I believe that he caught her from behind when she tried to run from him, and that's when he slashed her. Their story about what happened does not account for the blood pool on the side of the house," finished Gunter.

"As you know, Robert, Mrs. Beach plans to testify for the defense on her husband's behalf, and as you also know, as the prosecuting attorney you cannot compel a wife to testify against her husband. With the victim testifying for the perpetrator, we may never convince the jury of his guilt," added Baughn.

"Yes, you are right. Once passion cools and reason returns, people act quite differently. Combine this with millions in wealth and the perspective changes once the heat passes. But if she does testify for the defense, it opens up my opportunity to cross-examine her, and I will have poignant questions for her then," said Gunter.

The Trial
February 4–5, 1913

Judge Spain was brought in from Darlington to preside at the trial of South Carolina vs. Frederick Beach in the Aiken County Court of General Sessions. The selected jury consisted solely of men who were primarily farmers.

The courtroom was filled to capacity, and indeed seats were selling for $2 each. Such was the fascination that gripped Aiken's population for the "Trial of the Century." Despite the sensationalism that accompanied this event, the winter colony residents in general showed a lack of interest in the trial with the exception of a few of Beach's close friends, Mrs. C. Oliver Iselin and Clarence Dolan. Mrs. Beach sat dutifully with her husband in the courtroom and they held hands.

For the defense, Colonel Henderson planned to bring only three witnesses to testify: Miss Marion Hollins, Mrs. Beach, and possibly Mr. Beach.

Solicitor Gunter had an array of witnesses he planned to call. Miss Hollins, Mayor Gyles, Dr. Hastings Wyman, Dr. Marion Wyman, and sister Lallah would testify as to the screams in the Allison and Turner lots. Miss Wyman also would testify as to seeing the gray-suited man running from the scene. Dr. Hastings Wyman would testify as to the human blood found on Beach's penknife. Mayor Gyles would testify as to receiving the gold penknife from its owner, Frederick Beach. News reporter Johnson would testify as to overhearing the conversation concerning Robert Bronson between husband and wife while Johnson was hiding behind the bookcase.

Additionally, Solicitor Gunter assembled a small group of minor witnesses made up of servants and housemaids from the Beach and Lyons' homes who made observations on the night of the attack. Police Chief Howard and Officer Holley were also scheduled to be examined as to their observations.

The trial lasted two days, and there is no existing transcript of the actual testimonies given; our information is based on contemporary newspaper reports.

In outlining his case, Solicitor Gunter discounted the assumption that a Negro cut Mrs. Beach's throat. He asserted that the prosecution had "eliminated everyone upon whom the defense had endeavored to lay the crime."

"Mr. Beach's lawyers have asked for a theory, for a motive. If they want it, I will give it to you," said Gunter to an enrapt courtroom audience. "I tell you," he thundered, "the green-eyed monster, jealousy, will cause men to do things that may seem unaccountable." With this introduction, Gunter plunged into a recital which brought color into Mrs. Beach's face. Gunter continued, "Mr. Beach wasn't after Mrs. Beach when he tore that paling off the fence and ran around the sidewalk: He was after the man that Miss Wyman saw run out of the gate of the laundry enclosure and down Hood's Lane, after he (Beach) had run into that gate and encountered Pearl Hampton, knocking her down with the paling, and she screamed, giving the alarm!" The courtroom was draped in silence as Gunter finished explaining his theory of what took place on the night of February 26, 1912.

Dr. Wyman's testimony became somewhat tentative when asked about the knife blades by the defense. The chemist who tested the knife blade for human blood became less than positive when closely questioned by the defense team. Their tentativeness as witnesses did not help the prosecution's effort.

Camilla Beach did testify on her husband's behalf. The fact that she was the victim and would not testify against the alleged assailant was extremely damaging.

"Did you ever hear of a case of assault and battery in which the person who was assaulted was not put on the witness stand by the prosecution?" Colonel Henderson asked the jury.

"We usually argue the evidence," said W. Q. Davis, a member of the defense team to the jury. "Here we must argue the lack of it."

After one hour forty-five minutes, Jury Foreman A. H. McCarrell handed the verdict to John W. Dunbar, clerk of the court, who announced the verdict—Frederick Beach not guilty of assault and battery with intent to kill.

According to *The New York Times*, "Beach smiled upon hearing the verdict. He shook hands with each of his lawyers and with the four jurors seated on the front row, waving his hand to include the rest, then shook hands with Judge Spain. Mr. Beach received from the court stenographer his gold-handled diamond-studded pocket knife, and then went to the foreman of the jury, shook hands with him, and slapped him on the back."

Local newspapers speculated that Mrs. Beach's denial that her assailant was her husband was a key testimony influencing the jury. She never wavered from her original statement blaming an unknown Negro male as her attacker. Her testimony overcame any strong circumstantial evidence offered by Solicitor Gunter.

Thus ended Aiken's "Trial of the Century."

THE REST OF THE STORY

Camilla Havemeyer Beach remained married to Frederick O. Beach until his death in 1918 and never remarried. She died of a heart attack in her apartment in the Hotel Pierre at Sixty-first Street and Fifth Avenue in New York City on November 8, 1934 at the age of sixty-five. Her personal wealth and what she inherited from her late husband's estate passed on to her children: Theodore A. Havemeyer II of Vancouver, BC, Charles F. Havemeyer of New York, by her first marriage with Charles Havemeyer, and Frederick O. Beach, Jr. of New York, and John A. Beach of Santa Cruz, California.

Frederick O. Beach's charge of assault and battery with intent to kill was not a felony in South Carolina in 1912. Following his indictment it was reported in certain newspapers that he was given an opportunity to enter a guilty plea in exchange for paying a $100 fine, which he refused, opting to defend his honor and good name.

Following his ordeal, he continued to visit Aiken and was a devotee of polo and coach driving for the remainder of his life.

He died at the age of sixty-two in 1918. At the time of his death, he was still a partner in the Stock Exchange firm of Tailer & Robinson. His wealth passed on to his widow Camilla.

Robert L. Gunter was in his third year as solicitor of the Second Judicial Circuit at the time of the Beach trial. He continued to serve another eleven years. Prior to that time he represented Aiken in the state legislature 1901–1902, following which he became Aiken's county attorney. He was a commissioner of the city's water works at the time of the present system's installation. In addition to his other civic accomplishments, he was chairman of the board of the Aiken County Hospital.

On Sunday morning, October 27, 1940, while sitting in his chair at home reading his morning newspaper, he was stricken with a heart attack and died. He is buried in Bethany Cemetery, Aiken.

M. S. Baughn left Aiken following the trial and continued as a special detective, working primarily in the state of Georgia. It was reported that in the 1920s, he took part in the seizure of a large illegal liquor shipment (eighty barrels of whiskey) in Macon, Georgia, in the enforcement of Prohibition laws. Baughn never returned to Aiken as far as is known, and nothing further is known of the remainder of his life.

Sources

Articles

"A History of Hopelands Gardens," Aiken County Historical Museum, 1979.

"Hope Iselin/C Spear Ranch/Cliff House," Aiken County Historical Museum.

"Aiken Has Ties to the Titanic Tragedy," *The Aiken Standard*, January 28, 2011.

"Aiken Hospital Near Completion," *The Journal and Review*, November 22, 1916.

"Aiken Hospital Opens This Week," *The Journal and Review*, May 16, 1917.

"Aiken Hospital The City's Pride," *The Journal and Review*, May 2, 1917.

"Aiken's Hotel," *The Augusta Chronicle*, February 26, 1898.

America's Cup, Wikipedia.

"Beach Acquitted; Charges Conspiracy," *The Augusta Chronicle*, February 8, 1913.

"Beach and Wife Deny That He Slashed Her," *The New York Times*, February 7, 1913.

"Beach Charged with Cutting Wife's Throat," *The Augusta Chronicle*, April 9, 1912.

"Beach Coming Back; Asks Speedy Trial," *The New York Times*, April 13, 1912.

"Beach Gives Bond to Answer Charges," *The New York Times*, April 12, 1912.

"Beach Much Shaken Hurries To Paris," *The New York Times*, April 10, 1912.

"Beach Ready for Trial," *The New York Times*, January 30, 1913.

"Beach Trial Goes Over Till February," *The New York Times*, September 3, 1912.

"Beach Trial Opens Today," *The New York Times*, February 4, 1913.

"Begin Beach Trial at Aiken Tuesday," *The Augusta Chronicle*, February 3, 1913.

"Busy Day on the Links," *The New York Times,* September 11, 1898.

"C. Oliver Iselin, Noted Banker, Dead," *The New York Times*, January 2, 1932.

"C.O. Iselin's Son Dead," *The New York Times*, September 6, 1909.

"Capt. Herreshoff Boat Builder Dead," *The New York Times*, June 3, 1938.

Charles Oliver Iselin, Wikipedia.

"Col. William Goddard," Obituary, *The New York Times*, September 21, 1907.

"Death of C. F. Havemeyer," *The New York Times*, May 11, 1898.

"Destruction Highland Park Hotel Foretold," *The Augusta Chronicle*, February 21, 1898.

Ernest Schelling, Wikipedia.

"Family Gets Bulk of Iselin's Estate," *The New York Times*, January 8, 1932.

Flying Ace, Wikipedia.

"Four Are Saved in Philadelphia Family," *The Washington Times*, April 19, 1912.

"Friends Stood by Beach, Insisted on Sharing with Him the $10,000 Expense of Trial," *The New York Times*, February 9, 1913.

George D. Widener, Jr., Wikipedia.

George Dunton Widener, Wikipedia.

"Goddard Family Paper," Rhode Island Historical Society Manuscripts Division, 1997.

Harry Elkins Widener, Cyclopaedia of American Biography.

"Has More Beach Evidence. So Says Detective – Prosecutor Objects to Defense Helping Free Witnesses," *The New York Times*, April 11, 1912.

"Highland Park Hotel Licked Up By Flames," *The Augusta Chronicle*, February 7, 1898.

"Highland Park Hotel Theatre," *The Aiken Courier-Journal*, February 12, 1876.

"Highland Park Site For Sale," *The Augusta Chronicle*, February 19, 1898.

"Highland Park," *The Aiken Courier-Journal*, November 27, 1875.

"Hitchcock Killed In Crash In Britain," *The New York Times*, April 20, 1944.

"Hon. William H. Taft Will Arrive Today," *The Augusta Chronicle*, April 9, 1914.

"Hope Goddard Engaged to C. O. Iselin," *The New York Times*, May 6, 1894.

"Hope Goddard Iselin," Aiken Thoroughbred Racing Hall of Fame & Museum.

Hope Goddard Iselin, Wikipedia.

"Hope Goddard Married To Mr. Iselin," *The New York Times*, June 10, 1894.

"Hopelands – 135 Dupree Place," *The Aiken Standard*, April 15, 1971.

"Hotel Burned At Aiken, S.C.," *The New York Times*, February 7, 1898.

"How Astor Fortune Is Fixed," *The New York Times*, April 23, 1912.

"Improvements Completed and Nearing Completion," *The Journal and Review*, November 17, 1897.

"Iselin a Woman of the Sea," Jeffery B. Wallace, *The Aiken Standard*, November 18, 2006.

"Iselin Favors Lynching: Defends Frederick O. Beach, Target of Gossip in Aiken, SC," *The New York Times*, March 12, 1912.

"John Jacob Astor Was Born at New York Mansion Yesterday," *The New York Times*, August 15, 1912.

John Lyman Chatfield, Wikipedia.

Joseph E. Widener, Wikipedia.

"Local Affairs," *The Aiken Courier-Journal*, June 17, 1876.

"Local Affairs," *The Aiken Journal*, April 11, 1874.

"Local Affairs," *The Aiken Journal*, August 29, 1874.

SOURCES

"Local Affairs," *The Aiken Journal*, March 28, 1874.

"Magnificent Memorial Will Be Unveiled Today in Honor of the Late Major Archibald W. Butt," *The Augusta Chronicle*, April 14, 1914.

"Major Archibald Butt Is Lost the Reluctant Conclusion of President Taft Last Night," *The Augusta Chronicle*, April 17, 1912.

"Marion Hollins Witness at the Trial of Beach," *The Augusta Chronicle*, February 4, 1913.

"Memorial to Major Archibald W. Butt Most Fitting Honor to a Brave Man," *The Augusta Chronicle*, April 20, 1914.

"Mistakes of the Valkyrie," *The New York Times*, November 6, 1893.

"Mix Beach Witness On Knife Testimony," *The New York Times*, February 6, 1913.

"Mr. Goddard's Will Filed," *The New York Times*, September 28, 1907.

"Mrs. Beach Beside Husband at Trial," *The New York Times*, February 5, 1913.

"Mrs. Beach Smiles at Compliment to Her in Testimony by Dr. Hastings Wyman," *The Augusta Chronicle*, February 5, 1913.

"Mrs. Charles Iselin, Turf Figure and Social Leader, Dies at 102," *The New York Times*, April 6, 1970.

"Mrs. Frederick O. Beach Daughter of the Late C. D. Moss Had Heart Attack," *The New York Times*, November 9, 1934.

"Mrs. Laughlin Wed to T. Hitchcock, Jr.," *The New York Times*, December 16, 1928.

"Mrs. William H. Taft's Tribute to Major Archibald W. Butt," *The Augusta Chronicle*, April 15, 1914.

Nathanael Greene Herreshoff, Wikipedia.

Nieuport II, Wikipedia.

"Only One Ground Says Mr. F. O. Beach," *The Augusta Chronicle*, April 11, 1912.

"Philadelphians On Board. All Prominent Socially – Mr. & Mrs. George D. Widener Among Them," *The New York Times*, April 16, 1912.

"Planting the Centennial Tree," *The Aiken Courier-Journal*, April 22, 1876.

"Pocket Knife Before Court in Beach Trial," *The Augusta Chronicle*, February 6, 1913.

"Reception at the New Aiken Hospital," *The Journal and Review*, May 23, 1917.

"Robert Gunter Dies Suddenly," *The Aiken Standard and Review*, October 30, 1940.

"Saluting the Vigilant," *The New York Times*, October 15, 1893.

"Say F. O. Beach Attacked Wife," *The New York Times*, April 9, 1912.

Second Battle of Fort Wagner, Wikipedia.

"Solicitor Claims Prima Facie Case Against Frederick Beach; His Lawyers Expect An Acquittal," *The Augusta Chronicle*, February 14, 1913.

St. Paul's School, Wikipedia.

"The Highland Park Hotel," *The Augusta Chronicle*, March 31, 1899.

"The Highland Park Hotel," *The Journal and Review*, December 2, 1896.

"The Livery Business," *The Journal and Review*, April 6, 1892.

"The Memorial Dedication to Major Butt April 14th," *The Augusta Chronicle*; from *The Washington Star*.

"The New Hospital," *The Journal and Review*, May 23, 1917.

"The Titanic Musicians," *The New York Times*, April 22, 1912.

"Thousands Join In Tribute to Maj. Butt," *The Augusta Chronicle*, April 16, 1914

"Thrilling Tale By Titanic's Surviving Wireless Man," *The New York Times*, April 28, 1912.

"Titanic Survivor Hurt. W. E. Carter, Thrown in Bryn Mawr Polo Game, Lands on His Head," *The New York Times*, June 6, 1912.

"Titanic Survivors Asking $6,000,000, Well-Known Names Missing," *The New York Times*, January 16, 1913.

"Titanic Ties," *The Aiken Standard*, April 15, 1998.

"To Defend America's Cup, C. Oliver Iselin to Head the Syndicate and Manage the Boat," *The New York Times*, January 18, 1895.

"To Try Beach In February. New York Man Must Face Charge of Assault on Wife," *The New York Times,* January 8, 1913.

"Town and County News," *The Aiken Tribune*, October 11, 1873.

"Victory for the Vigilant," *The New York Times*, October 14, 1893.

Vigilant (yacht), Wikipedia.

"Wife Sues W. E. Carter: Philadelphia Society Couple Saved From Titanic Want Divorce," *The New York Times*, January 31, 1914.

"William Carter's Account," *The Evening Telegram*, April 22, 1912.

"William E. Carter Divorced; Wife Gets Decree at Philadelphia – Both Titanic Survivors," *The New York Times*, June 16, 1914.

"William E. Carter Succumbs to Illness," *West Palm Beach Inquirer*, March 21, 1940.

"William E. Carter, Titanic Survivor, Polo Player Before World War, Dies in Florida," *The New York Times*, March 21, 1940.

William E. Carter, Titanic Survivor, Encyclopedia Titanica.

William Larimer Mellon, Sr., Wikipedia.

Windham Wyndham-Quin, 4th Earl of Dunraven and Mount Earl, Wikipedia.

"Winter Resort, The Highland Park Hotel," *The Aiken Tribune*, February 13, 1875.

Books

Aldrich, Nelson W., Jr. *Tommy Hitchcock An American Hero*. Fleet Street Corporation, 1984.

Brewster, Hugh. *Gilded Lives, Fatal Voyage; The Titanic's First-Class Passengers and Their World*. New York: Crown Publishers, 2012.

Byrdy, Stan. *Augusta and Aiken in Golf's Golden Age*. Charleston, SC: Arcadia Publishing 2002.

Gracie, Colonel Archibald. *The Truth About the Titanic*. New York: HarperCollins Publishers, Inc., 2012.

Kaplan, Justin. *When the Astors Owned New York; Blue Bloods and Grand Hotels in a Gilded Age*. New York: Penguin Group, 2006.

Kaye, Elizabeth. *Lifeboat No. 8; An Untold Tale of Love, Loss, and Surviving the Titanic*. San Francisco: Byliner Inc., 2012.

Lawrence, Kay. *Heroes, Horses & High Society.* Columbia, SC : The R. L. Bryan Company 1971.

Lord, Walter. *The Night Lives On.* New York: Avon Books, 1987.

Olson, Lynne. *Citizens of London.* New York: Random House, 2010.

Pastore, Christopher. *Temple to the Wind: The Story of America's Greatest Naval Architect and His Masterpiece Reliance.* Guilford, Connecticut: The Lyons Press, 2005.

State of South Carolina v. Frederick O. Beach. Indictment bundle 179. SC Department of Archives & History

Tromp, Marlene. *Untold Titanic: The True Story of Life, Death, and Justice.* ISBN: 9781620954751.

ALSO BY David M. Tavernier

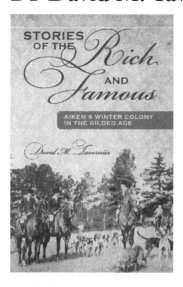

Stories of the Rich and Famous

Aiken was a small, relatively obscure southern town until the arrival of an aristocratic New Orleans family with strong societal ties. And it didn't take long before there was a seasonal flood of winter visitors—with names like Hitchcock, Vanderbilt, Whitney, and Astor. This South Carolina town was drawing the country's wealthiest and most powerful families, beginning in the 19th century and continuing on past World War II. Every fall they came by private railcar to play polo and golf, race thoroughbreds, and hunt fox. They held high tea, musicales, balls, and dinners, and every spring the "Winter Colony" migrated north again, leaving behind mansions and traditions that still resonate in Aiken 100 years later.

Author David M. Tavernier has woven a fascinating collection of stories around the people and places of this era. Based on fact, fiction, and years of historical research, the stories of "the Newport of the South" are masterfully and vividly brought to life.

**Learn more at: www.outskirtspress.com/
storiesoftherichandfamous**

CPSIA information can be obtained
at www.ICGtesting.com
Printed in the USA
LVHW080954251022
731507LV00020B/218